BEECH BANK GIRLS IV

Beech Bank Girls IV

A Time
Remembered

ELEANOR WATKINS

DERNIER PUBLISHING

London

To my newest
granddaughter, Cerys Eleanor,
with much love

Contents

PART ONE

Willow's Story

SAYING GOODBYE

one

The New Year kicked off to a flying start. Christmas had been great. We'd had a fab party at Beech Bank and the Big Freeze had stayed all through the holidays. We were able to go sledging every day and even try a bit of skiing, which was fun. It was good to start a new school term and a new beginning of sessions at Beech Bank, our cool after-school club.

After that, the year seemed to rapidly go downhill somehow. To begin with, there was a thaw. Not a dramatic one, with water pouring off the hillsides and big chunks of ice floating down the river, but a slow, sludgy, depressing kind of affair, with the snow turning grey and soggy, sludgy mud on all the pavements. The kind of weather when you can't wear decent boots, or they'd be ruined in no time.

But, worse than that, *far* worse, was what happened to Granddad.

"I just can't bear to send him back to that place," said Mum, stashing away the Christmas decorations for another year. "Here, Willow, untangle these lights, could you?"

She handed me a sad-looking tangle of green plastic wire and small glass bulbs, which until recently had twinkled magically, sparkling like stars among a mass of evergreen. Mum is an artist and very creative with Christmas decorations. She really hates seeing the tree and decorations go, so we're always ages behind everyone else taking them down. Now everything looked drab and depressing; tacky tinsel lay in heaps and browning evergreen dropped dead leaves and needles all over the floor.

I couldn't bear it either. Granddad had stayed over Christmas, and it had been great. He was confused these days, but that didn't stop him having a good time and a laugh. It was extra work for all of us but we'd got into a kind of routine and didn't mind.

Except that now my brother and I were back at school and Dad at work, it was Mum who had most of the responsibility. Granddad had been living in an old people's home for a while now, and was due to go back very soon.

"I can't bear it," repeated Mum, piling baubles into a box. "He doesn't complain much, but I'm sure he doesn't like it there."

"If only . . ." I began, and then stopped. Granddad was my dad's father, not my mum's, and I knew Dad felt a bit awkward about Mum having to take most of the responsibility for his care. I wasn't sure it would be fair on Mum either.

Mum looked at me across the box of festive stuff.

"You know, I'm sure we could manage if he stayed with us. There's a day centre in town where he could go mornings, and stay for a hot lunch. We'd just have him afternoons and weekends. He'd be much happier. What do you think?"

I wanted to hug her. "Mum, I think it's a wonderful idea! We'll all help!"

So it was arranged. Mind you, there were problems from the start. Bedrooms, for one. We only have three, and over Christmas, my little brother Rowan had given up his room for Granddad. There'd been a bit of a fuss about it, and I felt ashamed thinking about my part in it. My room is quite big, and Mum had wanted to screen off part of it and put a bed in there for Rowan, just temporarily. I wasn't having it. My room is my refuge, I've decorated it myself, all blue and silver, and it's all just as I want it. The idea of a snotty-nosed little eight-year-old putting his sticky fingers all over my things, even for a short time, made me feel quite ill. So Rowan ended up on the sofa bed in Dad's study downstairs. He was quite cheerful about it, though Dad had a few worries about his neat and tidy paperwork and office stuff.

"It's only for sleeping," Mum told him. "All Rowan's things can stay in the old room, and he can play in there in the daytime when Granddad's up and about."

So that's how it was. We fell into a routine, Mum dropping off Granddad at the day centre on the way to the shops, and fetching him after lunch. There wasn't time for her painting any more, and I did sometimes notice her looking wistfully at the stacked canvases in her little work room. But she never complained. And Granddad seemed happy. It was working out.

Until that Tuesday. I came home from Beech Bank Club and found a scene of pandemonium. All the lights were blazing inside and out, a most unusual thing as Mum and Dad are always trying to conserve energy and save the planet. The front door was open and worst of all, an ambulance stood outside, blue lights flashing. My heart seemed to stop, then start hammering hard, and I ran the last few yards to the house, reaching the front gate at the same time as two ambulance men with a long shape on a stretcher. Granddad's pale face and white hair was all I could see; the rest of him was covered with a red blanket. As I stood gaping on the pavement, they slid the stretcher efficiently into the vehicle, and my dad jumped in as well. Then they were gone, lights flashing and siren blaring.

My mum was there beside me suddenly, putting her arm round me, and I saw Rowan in the doorway, outlined against the hall light.

"Willow, I'm sorry, I meant to call you before you got here but it was such a rush getting things together . . ."

My legs were trembling. "What happened?"

"He – he decided he was going for a walk before tea. I told him it wasn't a good idea, and sat him down with Rowan to play draughts. Your dad was due home. I just went in the kitchen for a few minutes, but he must have decided he was going anyway – I heard the door open and then a kind of thump and a shout – he only got as far as the doorstep, must have slipped." She was crying now and I could feel her shivering. Rowan was blubbering too. I steered them both inside and shut the door.

Mum pulled herself together. "The ambulance came very quickly, so did your dad. They gave him a shot of morphine – said his hip was probably broken. He was in a lot of pain . . ." Her lips trembled again. It had been a terrible shock. My hands were shaking too, but I filled the kettle and switched it on, wondering briefly why people always make a cup of tea in a crisis. Something to do, I suppose. And plenty of sugar, for shock. I filled up the sugar bowl and tried to speak reassuringly.

"They'll know what to do in the hospital, Mum. I'm sure they must have fixed lots of broken hips."

The kettle boiled and I put teabags into mugs. Mum took hers gratefully, and even managed a smile. "Thanks, love. I just hope he won't hate being in hospital. Or that it won't make him more confused. I know he's not my dad, but he's such an old sweetie . . ."

That made me lose it, too. For a few moments the three of us sniffed and sobbed in between sips of tea, hating the thought of Granddad being in pain, and maybe scared, not knowing what was going on.

two

Sometimes I feel sorry for people who don't have a Beech Bank Club in their lives. Or wonder how we managed before we had one here. I mean, how boring would it be if we just had to go straight home after school?

Beech Bank is the best thing ever. Everything you need is there – a quiet place to do homework or chat, somewhere to listen to music, a big room for special events, computers, coffee and chill-out space. And always a listening ear if you need one.

I went there with the others the day after Granddad was taken into hospital. But not before I'd phoned home for the latest update. Mum said he'd had the hip pinned and was in recovery. She and Dad were going to visit later. But no, maybe not a good idea for Rowan and me to go just yet. He'd be very woozy and tired. Maybe tomorrow. I was disappointed about that but kind of relieved too, which made me feel a bit guilty.

"I didn't think I'd be so wimpy," I said to Annie and Chloe as we got some coffees. "But I just can't bear the thought of seeing Granddad in pain."

"That doesn't make you wimpy," said Chloe. "We'd

all be the same. I don't like it when Peter's in hospital. Men look so pathetic, stuck in bed and kind of helpless. Especially in those hospital gown things."

Her older brother Peter has a serious condition and has to go into hospital from time to time. And he's only a couple of years older than us. I'd forgotten.

"Sorry, Clo," I said. "Must be much worse for you and your family."

She gave me a hug. "Don't be silly. But don't worry too much. They'll look after him. And they'll give him stuff for the pain."

I hugged her back and wondered whatever I'd do without my mates. The rest of them came over from the homework room where they'd been using the computers. Holly had a new haircut, a short bob, which dipped forward over her cheeks as she bent forward. Amber and Rachel were discussing some dog-training classes they were thinking of going to. I felt myself relax. Everything would be all right.

It wasn't though.

I gave BB a miss next day and bounced in the door at home, feeling normal again. I was looking forward to having tea, whipping through homework, then getting ready to go and see Granddad.

I could see at a glance that Mum wasn't very happy, putting a meal together in the kitchen. "Granddad's not so well," she said.

"Oh Mum, does that mean that we still can't go and visit?"

She shook her head. "No, we'll all go and see him. But he's not doing as well as hoped. He has a touch of pneumonia. It sometimes happens when elderly people have accidents and are immobilised."

The worried, sick feeling came back again.

Granddad looked very pale in the hospital bed, propped up on pillows, with a frame keeping the bedclothes from weighing on him. He had a drip in his hand and an oxygen thing up his nose. He tried to be cheery for us, but his breathing seemed difficult and trying to talk brought on a cough. I felt tears well up, and tried to blink them back. After we'd all greeted him, Mum pushed Rowan and me forward. "Talk to him. Tell him what you've been doing in school today."

So I swallowed the lump in my throat and told him bits about the day, trying to keep my voice from quavering. It was pretty boring stuff, double French, maths, netball practice – although I tried to think of funny things, like Lucy Forrester making a mistake in a French phrase so that it came out really rude. Rowan told him about the goals he'd scored – I thought he was fibbing because there couldn't possibly have been that many – but it was all good stuff if it amused Granddad. And he did seem amused, nodding and smiling, although he was getting mixed-up again and said, "Well done, Stanley!" because he was thinking we were his brother and sister and not his grandchildren. And then he had a bout of coughing.

Mum and Dad had gone off to speak to the Ward

Sister. They came back and sat with Granddad for a bit, and then the bell went for the end of visiting.

I sniffled a bit on the way home, although I don't cry as a rule. Mum tried to be reassuring. "He's getting antibiotics, and they're looking after him well. The pain is under control."

But I could tell from hers and Dad's faces that they were seriously worried, too.

Next day, the news was no better. The infection didn't seem to be responding to the antibiotics, so they were trying a different type.

"Maybe it would be better if just Dad and I visit this evening," said Mum when I phoned her at lunchtime. So I went to Beech Bank after school, feeling anxious and sad.

"Let's ask Sadie to pray with us about your granddad," said Annie when we'd finished homework. I had been praying, kind of – desperate prayers like, "Help Granddad, God," or "Please, please, *please*, let Granddad get better." Sadie, who is our Vicar's wife and runs Beech Bank with him, always says that anything we say to God, even silently in our minds, is praying, and she sometimes quotes somebody or other who once said, "Prayer is just a thought turned Godward." But she also says there's special strength and blessing when several people pray together in agreement. So I jumped at Annie's suggestion and wondered why we hadn't done it before.

Sadie was in the homework room with Hugh, one of the BB helpers, trying to sort out some glitch in a computer programme. But she came and sat with us after a bit.

Sadie is young and trendy, she has legs up to her armpits and cheekbones and brilliant style, though maybe a bit too eclectic for my taste. My mum and dad were hippy-dippy back in the day and I suppose I've reacted against it. I prefer classic understated elegance. But she's amazing. She already knew about Granddad and said she and Rod had been praying. "But let's pray together now," she said, and we all joined hands round the table. She prayed aloud, quite simply, thanking God for Granddad and what he meant to our family, and asking for relief from the pain and illness and for God's perfect will to be done in Granddad's life. All of us said "Amen!" which means, I've been told, "So be it".

Sadie gave me a hug as we got up to go. "Hang in there, Willow. You've got a strong faith. Just keep trusting. Remember, God loves your granddad even more than all of you do."

That was a comforting thought to take home. Of course God would work it all out. I went home feeling lighter-hearted than I had for days. Granddad would be getting better and back at home with us very soon, I was sure.

three

Granddad died.

I don't know how else to put it, though people use all those silly phrases like "passing over" or "passing away" or even just "passing", which is what Americans say. I know, because I have a boyfriend, kind of, who is American. The only other description of dying that makes any sense, to my mind, is "gone". Because that's how it seemed.

One day he was there, frail and poorly in the hospital bed, attached to more drips and tubes, but still able to smile and lift his hand to wave to us. The next he was gone. They said his heart gave out in the end. And that he wasn't in pain. That he died peacefully. None of it helped. He wasn't there any more. My wonderful, brave, sweet, bewildered, beloved Granddad. Grandma had left us and now Granddad had gone too.

Rowan cried buckets, and Mum was tearful too, inclined to reproach herself and say things like, "If only I'd stayed with him, he wouldn't have gone out and slipped," or, "we should have left him in the Home, where he'd have been safe."

Dad was the sensible one, even though he was closest to Granddad. Or maybe because of that. He said, "Let's be thankful he had a good, full life. That he wasn't ill for long. He didn't really like the Home, and sometimes he didn't understand what was going on. You did all you could for him, Honey, and more." And he and Mum hugged each other, and I think both of them were crying.

I cried too, at first, when I heard the news, but only for a bit. I couldn't believe it. And then I started to get angry. Questions buzzed in my mind. Why do people have to die when there are people they love and who love them – and don't want to be separated from? People who still need them. What's the point of living a long, full life if it's only going to end in death? What's the point of being born at all?

These angry thoughts buzzed around my mind all day and kept me awake at night. Most of all, though I didn't admit it even to myself at first, I was angry with God. Hadn't we prayed and trusted him to make Granddad well again? Wasn't he supposed to answer our prayers? If he didn't, or wouldn't, what was the point of praying at all? Didn't he hear, or didn't he care?

I was angry with the world too, for just carrying on as usual. People went to work and school, everyone I saw in the street looked normal and even happy, some of them laughing and chatting without a care in the world. How could they do that, when my world had fallen to pieces?

It was Chloe, sweet caring Chloe, who got through

to me. Mum made us go to school next day, which I thought was cruel but which she said was better than sitting round moping and feeling sad.

"It gets better," said Chloe at lunchtime, when just the two of us were together for a few minutes. "I don't remember my mum dying, but think about Rachel and her dad. She remembers, and they got through that time. And Holly's grandma died, and she coped. And remember what a drama there was when Amber's dog died. But she got through that as well."

I managed a weak grin, thinking about Amber and her dramas, and felt a bit better. But the anger and the questions were still there. I didn't want to go to Beech Bank either but the others dragged me along. Sadie took one look at my face and pulled me into the quiet room.

"You look as though you need to get something off your chest."

And then I burst into tears and everything came spilling out. Sadie waited, and listened, and squeezed my hand, and handed me a box of tissues for mopping.

"Why didn't God let Granddad get well, when we prayed?" I ended, on a note that sounded more like a wail.

She didn't answer that for a minute or two. Then she said, "Willow, we don't altogether understand how prayer works. Or what God's will is. We did ask him to do what's best for your granddad, remember?"

I sat up straight. "Yes, but I meant for him to get well and come home. It's not fair."

I realised how childish I was sounding; me, Willow, the one who's the leader and always in control. Sadie smiled. "Life isn't fair. Or death. God never meant for it to happen, but it did, because of sin coming into the world. We understand very little of why things happen as they do. But we have Jesus with us to help us through life. We know your granddad's safe with Jesus now, and he's not old or ill or confused any more. We must remember the good, happy years he's had. And in the end, '*all will be well, and all will be most well, and all manner of things will be well.*' Those are the words of a very wise woman who lived a long time ago, and lived very close to God."

I thought, not for the first time, that Sadie was a very wise woman herself. She squeezed my hand again. "It will get better, I promise. In the meantime, it's OK to cry, and shout, and be angry at God if that's how you feel. He understands and can cope with it. You can ask why if you like, but don't expect an answer. Just remember he'll never leave you."

She leant across and gave me a big hug. I mopped some more. She said, "Try and bear up for your mum and dad and Rowan. They'll be feeling just like you." I nodded. I would. I got up to go. "And, Willow," she said, "maybe it would help to have a chat with Jay. Just a thought."

Jay! I'd almost forgotten him in the upsets of the last few days. Just the mention of his name gave my heart a lift. I'd text him as soon as I got home and arrange a Skype date.

four

I did talk to Jay, and it was strangely comforting to see his face with the lock of floppy hair falling over his forehead, and to hear his voice, even though it doesn't sound quite the same on Skype. He said he was very sorry and that he'd liked Granddad when he'd met him, which was only once. And then we talked about ordinary things; school, and holidays, and his family. I didn't cry or break down. It was all quite normal, and strangely reassuring.

It was the small, normal things that provided comfort over the next few difficult days. Dad was an only child, so it was he and Mum who had to make all the funeral arrangements. There was an awful lot of running around and signing things and phoning people. Mum bought new clothes for Rowan and me, suitably sombre for the occasion. I got a new long coat, quite a sophisticated one, which normally I'd have been thrilled about. Now what I wore didn't seem to matter in the least. I'd have gladly gone in my school uniform.

I decided it would help if I washed dishes and made beds, and made sure Rowan brushed his teeth and that kind of thing. Mum was very grateful; she's not organised at the best of times and she said she didn't know how she'd have managed without me. It gave me a lot of comfort too.

But the thing that helped most of all was that they found amongst Granddad's things a detailed account of how he wanted his funeral to be. Mum and Dad don't often go to church, and they'd been struggling to find suitable hymns and prayers and readings. Granddad, bless him, had written it all down, shortly after Gran's death and before the dementia had begun to set in. He wanted singing; joyful songs and lots of them. He'd picked out readings from the Bible, and a piece from the Episcopalian burial service that he wanted read at the graveside. He wanted to be buried next to Gran, and for Rod to speak at the service. He'd thought of everything.

All this made Mum tearful again. "It makes it so much easier for us. Just like Granddad, bless him!"

The day of the funeral was grey and dreary, but thank goodness it wasn't raining. I was glad it wasn't a lovely day with the sun shining and birds singing, though. I would have found that difficult. Grey and sad and sombre fitted better with my mood. We had the service at the little village church which Gran and Granddad had attended, not our St. John's, but Rod was there to help conduct it, and Sadie was there too. So, I was touched to see, were all my best mates, along with Rachel's mum, who must have packed them all into their 4x4. I hadn't realised they were all coming.

The little church was packed, not many relatives but

many, many neighbours and friends and even workers from the care home. Granddad had been well loved. That was comforting in itself.

Rowan and I walked behind Mum and Dad as they met the plain wood coffin and followed it into church, with some of my dad's cousins and aunts and uncles coming along behind. Rowan clutched my hand tight, something he hadn't done for a long time. One of Granddad's favourite pieces, *Jesu, Joy of Man's Desiring*, was being played as we got to the porch. Its lilting melody filled me with a strange kind of longing that the composer must have been feeling when he wrote it. And then it was replaced by Rod's strong voice as he went ahead of us. *"I am the Resurrection and the Life, he that believes in me, though he were dead, yet shall he live, and he that believes in me shall never die."*

A feeling of peace began to replace the weight of sadness in my heart. I'd been scared of crying and looking pathetic, but maybe I wouldn't. Maybe we'd get though OK.

It seemed strange and unreal though, sitting in the front pew and listening to people speak about Granddad, knowing that all the time he lay in that simple wooden coffin at the chancel steps. He had asked for family flowers only, and Dad and Mum's wreath of cream and green lilies lay alongside mine and Rowan's of early daffodils and hyacinths. Yet I knew he was not there. It was just his body, that worn-out part of him that wasn't needed any more.

Where was Granddad himself, the person, that kind, funny, gentle and courteous man we'd loved so much? Even now, I couldn't quite believe he'd gone. During the days between his death and the funeral I'd kept catching myself thinking I heard his voice or expecting him to be there smiling at me when I got in from school, mixing me up with his sister, saying, "Hello, Harriet. Had a good day?"

"Where are you, Granddad?" I whispered.

We sang all the songs Granddad had chosen – *There is a Redeemer*, *Amazing Grace*, *Oh for a Thousand Tongues* and others; joyful songs full of hope as he'd requested. I managed to read the short poem he'd chosen without my voice wobbling.

Rod spoke on love. How love is the thing that makes life worth living, and how Granddad's life had so well reflected that love. That love has many sides, and that one of them is pain and loss, but that it is worth paying the price. How love conquers many things: fear, disappointment, tragedy, even death itself. How God is pure love, and that now Granddad had entered fully into that love.

Rowan kept hold of my hand, and I realised that all four of us were holding hands tightly, sitting together in the front row. Then we were following the coffin again, out into the dull winter afternoon. It was a shock to see the open grave, with yards of horrible green plastic false grass laid out around it. Very final to see the coffin lowered into it.

Yet not final at all. We sang a verse of another hymn Granddad had chosen, *Shall we Gather at the River*, and Rod read the passage from the Episcopal service.

"You only are immortal, the creator and maker of mankind; and we are mortal, formed of the earth, and to earth we shall return. For so did you ordain when you created me, saying, 'You are dust, and to dust you shall return.' All of us go down to the dust; yet even at the grave we make our song: Alleluia, alleluia, alleluia."

As he read, his voice seemed to change from the solemnity of "dust to dust", until as he reached the final words it was as though he could no longer hold back the joy that these words promised. As he finished, a ray of sunshine broke through the grey sky and lit up the scene; the mourners in dark clothing, the open grave, the false grass, and the radiance on Rod's face as he proclaimed the final "Alleluia".

Rowan and I each had a long-stemmed lily, Granddad's favourite flower, to drop on to the coffin. Stepping forward, I felt a joy rise in my own heart to join the sense of peace and love, a joy that I knew was nothing to do with that thing we call happiness, which at best comes and goes and depends on circumstances, but everything to do with God, who had taken Granddad home to himself and had truly done all things well.

five

There are more things to do after someone dies than I'd ever have dreamed. More papers to sign. Affairs to be "wound up". Pensions to be cancelled, bank accounts to be closed, belongings to be disposed of. The closing down of an earthly life. All sad, final kinds of things. Dad and Mum would have preferred just to be quiet for a bit, coming to terms with the feelings of loss and the big space in our lives that Granddad left. Then again, maybe it was good for them to have things to do.

Granddad had left a will, of course, all legal and up-to-date. Most of what he had, which wasn't a lot in material terms, went to Dad and Mum, with some money for Rowan and me to be used if we went to uni or college, or some study or training course. This made my eyes fill with tears again. Dear Granddad, always watching out for us, planning ahead.

His house had been sold when he moved into the Home, but he'd been allowed to take some possessions with him. A few pieces of furniture he was specially fond of, for his room. His clothes, of course, his books and photos and personal things. It must have been hard for him, shrinking a lifetime of living and memories to make it fit into one not very large room. The room was needed now for someone else, of course, so we had the rather sad task of clearing everything out and bringing it home to be stored in the garage.

"We'll go through it all later, when things have had time to settle," said Mum, looking rather helplessly at the stacked boxes and packing cases that contained Granddad's earthly possessions. "Maybe I could fit that armchair into our bedroom, and I think the chest of drawers might be useful. Once we've emptied it, of course. At the moment it's stuffed full of Granddad's pullovers and socks and underwear. I expect most will go to charity, but I don't feel quite like sorting through it yet."

I knew what she meant. The idea of rummaging through Granddad's clothing, deciding which to discard, was something I wouldn't fancy myself.

"Can I have his chess set?" asked Rowan. "And that knife he used to make wooden animals and things with?"

Mum said yes to the chess set and no to the knife, although she said they'd keep it for when Rowan was older. Dad was inclined to disagree. "I always had a Scout knife when I was a kid and it never did me any harm. There were all kinds of things on it, corkscrew, different blades, and a thing for getting stones out of horses' hooves."

Mum gave him a look. "That was decades ago. Things

are different now. Boys and knives are not a good idea these days."

Rowan was in an argumentative mood. "But I might really want to do those things. I might *need* a knife."

"You won't," said Mum, and that was the end of it. She turned to me. "Is there anything you'd like, Willow? Books, maybe? Photos?"

I thought I'd like one or two of Granddad's books on trees and forestry. Jay's big passion is trees, and I might learn more myself. Granddad had kept photos on his table in the home, one of his and Grandma's wedding day, Grandma with a baby who was my dad, others of Dad as a boy and growing up, pictures of me and Rowan. I didn't think I wanted photos. Looking at them made me feel kind of sad at the moment.

Then my eye fell on the old trunk Granddad had kept beside his bed, with his lamp and glasses and whatever book he happened to be reading. It was a battered old thing, sturdy wood with metal bands and Granddad's name on the side. We'd looked in it briefly and saw it contained piles of paper stuff, more photos, notebooks, pamphlets, letters in bundles and school textbooks. It weighed a ton to move, and Dad had needed help with it. That trunk seemed to hold the essence of Granddad somehow.

"I'd like that," I said, pointing. "I'd like it in my room."

Mum looked surprised. "Are you sure? It won't fit with your décor at all."

It wouldn't, I knew. It would be totally out of place in my immaculate refuge. But I wanted it. Wanted to think of Granddad when I looked at it. Maybe, over time, I'd read some of the stuff inside and find out more about his life. So, with a lot of huffing and puffing, the trunk and contents were carried upstairs and installed in my room. I liked the look of it, solid and well-worn and slightly battered, like Granddad himself.

It was another week or so before I lifted the lid and looked at the stuff inside. I was amazed at the sheer volume of it, a lifetime of hoarding. It was real treasure though, as I rummaged through the top layers. Photos of Dad at all ages. Photos and sketches of trees. Sketched by Granddad? Bundles of letters. I opened one or two and saw they were love-letters between him and Grandma, in their courting days. No texts or emails in those days, just sweet, tender messages of love that brought tears to my eyes again. I put them back in the envelopes. I'd read more another day. Just now it seemed too much like an intrusion.

There were notebooks and exercise books from way back in Granddad's school days. I couldn't imagine wanting to keep my school stuff. He'd got top marks for essays but he wasn't very good at arithmetic, I noticed, just like me.

There were certificates from his teacher-training days, first aid ones, woodcraft awards, sailing qualifications, a special award for bravery. It didn't say what kind and he'd never spoken of it. And I'd hardly touched the top layer.

I delved down deeper, wondering what lay below, and pulled out a handful of stuff. A booklet about avoiding TB by living a healthy lifestyle. A brochure on different types of wood preservative. And another exercise book or notebook, quite small – or part of one – with the cover missing and half the book too. The flyleaf had a name in beautiful copperplate handwriting, *Grace Elizabeth Hebdon, Private Journal*. And a date, *July 29th 1914*.

I felt a flicker of excitement. Way before Granddad's day. Who was Grace Elizabeth Hebdon? I turned the page and found lines of the same beautiful handwriting.

Yesterday was a very important day, for two reasons. Firstly, it was my fourteenth birthday. This journal was one of my presents, and I hereby vow I will write in it every day. I had other gifts, lace-trimmed pillowslips from Mother, which she says are for my bottom drawer, and Father gave me a camera. Imagine! My very own camera! It is called a Box Brownie. I am not at all sure I will be able to use it but I will try. Carrie gave me a book, "Great Expectations", and Will gave me this journal, which I like best of all. I like the green cloth cover and the thick creamy pages to write on. I intend to write all my secrets, and my opinions, of which Father says I have far too many for a girl, and it will cause trouble for me if I don't watch out! Ha ha!

Mother made a cake for my birthday, and we had strawberries from the garden. Also cream, because Daisy calved last week and there's plenty of milk. We are making butter again, and I had to help, which I dislike. The salt and cold water makes my hands so red and chapped. Mother says I am altogether too particular for a farmer's daughter, and should marry into the gentry. Ha ha again!

The second important thing yesterday was that war has broken out. The postman told us this morning. I don't know really what it means, but I think it is fairly serious.

"Willow!" came Mum's voice from downstairs. "Tea's ready. I've called twice already."

I hadn't heard, having been swiftly drawn far away into another world, the world of Grace Elizabeth Hebdon and her family. I closed the book, and as I did so, noticed the corner of a photograph sticking out from between the pages further on. I pulled it out, turned it over and got a shock. My own face smiled up at me from the old, rather crumpled black and white photo. The girl in the picture was dressed in old-fashioned clothes, but the hair was the same, wild and curly, the nose, the forehead, the smile. She was tall and skinny just like me. I sat for a while with the photo in my hand. Was this Grace Elizabeth? And had she been someone in my own family? How had she been related, and what had happened to her? One thing was certain. I aimed to find out.

PART TWO

Annie's Story

COMING THROUGH

one

All of us went to Willow's granddad's funeral service. I didn't want to. I'd never been to a funeral before and I didn't know what to expect. Would everyone be crying and sobbing? Wouldn't it be just awful to know that there was a dead body in a coffin, right there in front of you? I'd heard that in some countries they had the coffin open, and everyone walked past to look at the dead person. That made me feel faint even to think about.

But I went, because all the others did, and I didn't want to look like a wuss. Rachel's mum offered to take us all in their massive people carrier, and said it would mean a lot to Willow for us to be there. In the end it wasn't too bad, not scary at all. The music they played was beautiful, kind of soaring up and lifting you with it. All the songs and prayers were full of hope, and promises about the next life. And I kind of knew, without knowing how I knew, that Willow's granddad was not really there in that long wooden box with flowers on top, but alive and happy somewhere else.

We girls stuck together in a group, holding hands or linking arms some of the time, for comfort. I only saw

the back of Willow's head in church, but when we got to
the graveside, Amber nudged me and whispered, "Look
at Willow!"

She looked absolutely stunning. Clothes always look
amazing on her, but she had a new coat on today, a proper
coat, not the padded chunky jackets we wear for school.
Black, and buttoned up to the neck, long and elegant and
fitting her like a glove. Above it, her face was paler than
usual and her red hair stood out like a sunburst. She just
stood with her family, tall and straight, not crying, and
when Rod said his piece with the "Alleluias", a gleam of
sun lit up her hair and she had the most amazing look
on her face. Like she was transformed, or something. I
started to cry, not really knowing why I was doing it, and
Chloe put her arm round me.

"It's nearly over, Annie," she whispered.

I was a bit nervous of speaking to Willow, but it was
OK. She came over and hugged us all, and we went round
to the church hall for tea and cakes and sandwiches. I
thought she'd be changed but she was still the same old
Willow.

We see a lot of each other, Willow and I, as we live
just round the corner from one another. Not only are
we friends, but our little brothers, Harry and Rowan, are
best buddies too. Very often Rowan is at our house, but
oftener still these days, Harry is at theirs. Because now
our mum has a Social Life.

"How do you feel about your mum going out with
Hugh?" Amber asked me curiously at Beech Bank one

day soon after the funeral. Both of us looked across at Hugh, who was shooting pool with some of the boys in the games area. I shrugged, stirring my coffee. I wasn't sure, really. I'd hated it when my mum and dad split up, and even more when Dad got a new girlfriend. I liked Hugh a lot, everyone here did. He had a steady kind of way with him, like you knew you could always depend on him in a crisis. I'd have thought him a bit dull, maybe, until Mum told me the amazing life he'd lived.

"I'm cool about it," I said, and hoped she'd drop the subject. "And she's not going out with him, exactly."

Amber raised an eyebrow. "No? Concerts, and meals, and little trips in the car? What would you call it then?"

I shrugged again. "Just being friendly. Maybe he's sorry for her. Or she's sorry for him."

Amber looked as though she was trying not to laugh. She said, "Yeah, whatever. They're both sorry for each other. If you say so."

I picked up my empty polka-dot mug and carried it to the sink. I didn't want to carry on with this conversation.

It wasn't that I minded, exactly. I knew Mum and Dad weren't happy even when they were still married. It had been a miserable time all round, last year. I'd been getting bullied at school and there was tension at home. When we'd moved here I'd really hoped everything would change. It did, for me, once I'd settled at Beechwood High and made friends. But then Mum told us the marriage was over. Worse came later, when it turned out that Dad had met someone else.

I really hated Samantha at first. Then things changed as I got to know her and found she's a really nice person, not a bit like I thought. And then there was Mum and Hugh. Ironically, they'd met at Beech Bank and hit it off from the start. Mum seemed suddenly to have come to life again.

Mind you, there are a few advantages to having parents who are separated. Two lots of pocket money for instance. I reckon parents in that situation feel guilty, so they give you more. Harry loves it, and I'm not complaining.

Dad spent Christmas with us, at Samantha's suggestion, sleeping on the sofa bed downstairs. It was OK, I guess. Loads of pressies, even more than usual. Mum cooking dinner, determinedly cheerful. Dad playing with Harry's new toys, the two of them shouting and hollering over some computer game. Me, scooting off to the service at St John's, to get out of the house and see my mates for a bit.

Hugh was there, in the congregation. Afterwards he came over to me.

"Happy Christmas, Annie. How's it going?"

He meant at home, I supposed. Not that it was any of his business.

"Having a lovely time, thanks," I said, rather stiffly.

"Great! Well, see you."

He smiled and wandered off. It did enter my head, just for a moment, to wonder if he was spending Christmas all alone. Not that I cared, of course.

After Christmas, it wasn't long before he and Mum were off out again, to an art exhibition somewhere or other. Then it was a meal at a new restaurant. Then something else. Mum bought a new outfit in the sales. I thought it was a bit young for her personally, but I had to admit she looked good in it. Dad was back with Samantha, and we were back to seeing him every other weekend, Harry and I. Christmas hadn't changed anything.

I must be having a bout of the winter blues or something, or that's what Chloe thought.

"Some people get it every year," she told me. "It's due to a lack of sunshine. They call it S.A.D.; Seasonal Affective Disorder. Some people have to go off every winter to tropical places to get sunshine."

"Nice for some people," I said.

I didn't think I had S.A.D. But I was sad. And after going to Willow's granddad's funeral and embarrassingly bursting out crying, I understood why. Seeing Willow's mum and dad standing at the graveside, their arms tightly round each other and the children, I'd realised that our family was never going to be like that again. Not ever.

two

Somehow, I couldn't seem to shake off the feeling of sadness. It was there when I woke up in the morning, like a big heavy lump in my middle. It stayed with me at school, at home, when I was with my mates, even at Beech Bank. I found myself bursting into tears, time and again, for no real reason, though I tried to do it when nobody else was around.

"Are you sure you're all right, Annie?" asked Mum one evening when we were actually watching a soap together for half an hour. "You've been looking a bit peaky lately."

"I'm fine," I said, trying to settle my face into what I hoped was a happy, carefree expression. I couldn't have succeeded, because a frown appeared between her eyes and she leaned across and brushed my hair back. "Are you sure, sweetie? You don't seem yourself somehow."

Suddenly, I wanted to bawl like a little kid and fling myself into her arms and sob and tell her I didn't know what was the matter really, that nothing was like it used to be, and sometimes I hated life . . .

But of course I couldn't say any of that. She'd only

blame herself and maybe stop seeing Hugh, and then I'd feel guilty, because that wasn't the problem really. Thing is, I had no idea what *was* the problem. Inspiration struck, and I bent and rubbed my ankle, which I'd badly sprained in a sledging accident before Christmas. It was better now, except for the odd twinge, but it was as good an excuse as any.

"My ankle hurts a bit now and then," I mumbled.

Mum seemed concerned. "Oh dear, I thought it had healed so well. I'll make an appointment for some more physio."

I sighed, but left it at that. My ankle was OK. It was the rest of me that was the problem really.

The other girls noticed that I was still a bit down. They tried to help, bless them. Willow said I should talk to Rod or Sadie, but I knew I'd end up bursting into tears. I was doing plenty of that already.

"What you need," decided Holly, "is a makeover. A nice, pampering weekend at a spa. There's one Mum and I go to . . ." and then she broke off, remembering that they weren't well-off any more and pampering spas were a thing of the past. If I'd wanted to, I could have afforded a spa weekend easily, or Dad would have forked out for it, but I didn't say anything. I didn't want to go to a spa anyway.

The others had jumped on the idea though. "We don't have to go to a fancy spa," said Amber. "We could do it ourselves, for next to nothing. Get lots of nice smelly things, do face packs, restyle our hair, paint our nails."

She peered at me. "How about changing your hair colour, Annie? A new look might give you a real lift. Maybe a hint of auburn?"

I didn't fancy that idea. I'd heard too many horror stories of girls trying new colours and it all going wrong, ending up with some hideous green or purple shade, or their hair coming out in clumps. Besides, I quite liked my own chestnut-brown, thick, shiny hair. "Maybe not," I said.

"Well, how about pierced ears?" suggested Amber, "You'd look good in long dangly earrings."

I gave that some consideration. All the other girls have pierced ears, and the earrings they sometimes wear do look nice. The little everyday studs are pretty cool too. There'd been a bit of a discussion at Beech Bank about body piercings and tattoos a while ago. Opinions were divided. Somebody found a Bible verse forbidding any such thing, then someone else pointed out that just a few verses earlier it was forbidden for men to cut their hair or trim their side whiskers. If you took one on board you had to take the lot, didn't you? Anyway, it had been more or less concluded that people should be guided by their own consciences. And that if we decided to have things done, we must always, always, go to a reputable trained and qualified person.

Which made what we *did* decide to do all the more mystifying, looking back on it. I'm not at all sure whose idea it was, or how I agreed to go along with it. I'd vaguely had an idea I'd get my ears pierced at some future date.

But here I was, a few days later, at Holly's house with all the others, except Willow, preparing to get a do-it-yourself ear piercing.

"It won't hurt," Holly assured me. "The ear lobe has very few nerve endings. A bit like hair or nails. They don't hurt when you cut them, do they?"

I wasn't convinced. I pinched my right ear lobe hard, and it hurt.

"Anyway," said Amber, "we'll freeze it first to deaden the sensation. We're doing everything properly. Trust us."

They had everything lined up on a clean white towel, a tumbler of ice-cubes, sterilised ear-studs, more sterilising fluid, a piece of cork, thin rubber gloves like surgeons wear, and most scary of all, a large darning needle.

Rachel and Chloe held ice cubes to my left ear lobe while Holly donned the gloves and sterilised the needle once again. My heart was beginning to thump and I wanted to jump up and get out of there. But that would make me look a real wimp.

"Now," said Holly, holding the needle, "just relax, close your eyes, and imagine yourself on a beach, in a white bikini, with an awesome tan and big gold hoops glinting in the sun."

I gulped. What I wanted very badly, all of a sudden, was just to forget it and go home, asap. I closed my eyes. Someone held my earlobe and then there was a sharp searing pain. I screamed.

The other girls backed off and I put my hand to my

ear. There was blood on my fingers. I started to struggle to my feet. The others were clustering round again to look, and I had this fleeting scary impression of a bunch of ghouls looking for blood.

"Annie, sit down," said Holly. "I haven't finished. I hardly got started. Now I'll have to sterilise the needle again."

"Don't bother," I said. "I've changed my mind. I don't want it done."

They seemed a bit disappointed, although Chloe at least had a concerned look too.

"It would have been all over in a moment," said Holly regretfully, "just a quick stab, and all done."

I shuddered. "No thanks. That really hurt." My ear was stinging. Rachel had a look at it. "Just a scratch, it's stopped bleeding. I'm really surprised it hurt so much. Wonder why the ice cubes didn't work?"

Holly seemed loath to give up, all geared up for the operation as she was.

"Would anyone else like their ears done?" she asked hopefully, needle poised.

The others declined. "Maybe it was a bit of a stupid idea after all," said Chloe.

"Willow would have thought so, if we'd told her," said Rachel.

"Good thing we didn't then."

"Are we going to say anything about it?"

We thought about it for a moment, and unanimously decided not.

three

No such thing as keeping anything quiet, where I live. Next day, my ear had started to throb, and when I looked in the mirror, the lobe looked very red. I made sure my hair was covering my ears and hoped for the best. Maybe it would settle in a day or two.

My mates don't miss a thing though. When I was bending forward, changing shoes for P.E., Chloe said suddenly, "Your ear looks a bit yuck, Annie. Does it hurt?"

It did, rather. Rachel was there too and she came to look. "Yikes, I think it's getting infected. You should see the doctor, Annie."

Willow and Amber had gone on ahead, but Holly came to see what the fuss was about. She took a look and went quite pale. "Oh, Annie, I'm so sorry! I was so careful with sterilising too. I wouldn't hurt you for the world."

There were tears in her eyes. The others were looking very solemn.

"Maybe it was a crazy thing to try and do ourselves," said Rachel. Holly nodded. "It was stupid. Annie, I'm really sorry. And there's me thinking I might be a beauty therapist!"

"We should have known better," said Chloe.

I thought we were all going to end up blubbering together. Rachel pulled herself together. "You must see the doc. Today. Or you might get blood poisoning. Ring and make an emergency appointment for afternoon surgery."

They all stood over me while I did. I'd have to go right after school and miss Beech Bank, but it couldn't be helped. The pain was beginning to spread to my whole ear.

There were footfalls outside the cloakroom and Miss Pierce burst in.

"What on earth are you girls doing? P.E. started ten minutes ago in the gym."

So then we had to explain, and Miss Pierce looked at my ear and tut-tutted and said what an irresponsible thing to do, she'd have expected better of us, and certainly I must see the doctor, blah blah blah, until we all felt about ten centimetres high.

The girls wanted to come with me to the surgery, but I thought questions would be asked at BB if we were all missing. As it was, Willow and Amber had to be told. Amber looked well ashamed, and Willow was incredulous.

"Well, honestly! That's the kind of thing Year Seven kids would do! What on earth were you thinking?"

We got the message.

By the time school ended, my ear was throbbing painfully. I wonder how long it took for blood poisoning to set in. I had a long wait at the surgery, having been squeezed in at the end. There are nine doctors in our practice and you never know who you're getting in emergency clinic. This evening it was Dr. Hartley. She looked at my ear, asked a question or two, and then checked the glands in my neck. She has rather a nice face, grey hair and laughter lines.

"Well, you've got the beginnings of an infection there sure enough. A short course of antibiotics should sort it out." She clicked on the computer screen, scribbled on the prescription pad. And then she swivelled her chair to face me and read me a lecture on the follies and risks of such things as attempting amateur beauty enhancements.

I couldn't help it. I knew only too well we'd all been stupid. The lump of misery inside me just rose up and choked me, and I burst into floods of tears.

Dr. Hartley propelled her wheelie chair towards me and took hold of my hands. "Hey, hey! It's not the end of the world. You'll be fine in no time with the antibiotics. You're not the first girl to get in this predicament and I don't suppose you'll be the last."

"It's not that," I sobbed. And then the whole story came tumbling out, the sadness and misery that wouldn't go away, the bullying at the old school, Mum and Dad breaking up, things changing so much when I wanted them to stay the same. She listened, and squeezed my hands, and passed me the box of tissues on her desk. Then she asked a few questions, listened again, and said "Annie, I think you have a touch of mild clinical depression. You have the classic symptoms."

I felt my mouth fall open in surprise. This was something I hadn't thought of.

"It's not uncommon among young people," she went on. "And it usually is a passing thing. From what you've said, your emotions have taken a battering over the last few months. And the ankle accident probably didn't help. There are things we can do to help."

I felt a load lift from my shoulders. The doctor really understood how I felt. She didn't tell me I was being silly or to pull myself together. I wasn't the only person my age who felt like this. I'd get better. They'd help me.

"The main thing," she said, "is to talk about things. Don't bottle everything up inside. I'll arrange a counsellor for you, but in the meantime, are there people you trust that you can talk to, and who'll listen?"

I thought of Beech Bank, and Sadie and Rod, and my mates, and nodded. "Yes. Yes, there are."

"Good. Then tell them how you're feeling. Don't feel you have to put on an act. You have nothing to be ashamed of."

I was feeling better already. Dr. Hartley found some leaflets about depression and went through them with me, and asked me a few more questions. Then she asked if there was anything I wanted to ask. I hesitated for a moment, not quite sure of the thing that had popped into my head. Then I said, "Doctor, is it OK if I ask people to pray for me?"

She looked surprised, and then nodded. "Yes. Yes, that's good. I'm not much of a praying person myself, but I've noticed with people in your situation that they often get better much quicker if prayer is involved. I've no idea how, but it does seem to work."

She glanced at her watch, which made me look at mine. I was amazed to find that over half an hour had passed. There were no sounds from the waiting room. The other patients must have been seen by someone else. Dr. Hartley had given me much more than the usual ten minutes or so of consultation time, and I was so grateful.

"You'll just catch the dispensary before it closes," she said, handing me the prescription for the antibiotics. "Come and see me again if you need to. I'll arrange the counselling. But no more DIY beauty therapies!"

I got to my feet. My ear was hurting quite badly but inside I felt a whole lot better. I'd get through this bad patch. Beech Bank would be almost over for today, but I couldn't wait to do what the doctor said and talk about everything to people I trusted. I'd start with the rest of the girls. I got my phone out and started to text.

four

The antibiotics worked fast, and soon not even a scar remained. All of us agreed we had been well stupid.

Of course I had to tell Mum everything, about the ear and about the depression. She wasn't too bothered about the ear-piercing episode, but was upset about the rest, as I knew she would be, and blamed herself.

"Annie, I'd no idea you were feeling like that. I'm so sorry. I've been starting to enjoy life again, and not spending enough time with you. I knew you were feeling down, but never guessed . . ." She looked as though she might burst into tears herself.

I said quickly "Mum, Mum, it's OK. It's not your fault. I want you to enjoy life. I'm feeling better myself already."

And I was. Now that I could talk openly about how I felt, half the misery had melted away.

Sadie and the girls were amazing, surrounding me with love. "You know," said Sadie one afternoon at Beech Bank, "I think this whole episode is a prime example of the 'all things'."

I was puzzled. "What do you mean?"

Sadie fetched her Bible and leafed through it, finding a chapter in the New Testament. "Here we are. Romans 8, verse 28. Listen to this, *'And we know that in all things God works for the good of those who love him, who have been called according to his purpose.'*"

She closed the Bible. "Think about it. It was because you were feeling down that the girls tried to help you with home beauty treatments." She smiled. "Obviously they went about it the wrong way. But God knows our intentions, and he can transform even the mistakes and bad things and turn them into good. You had to go to the doctor and she spotted the real problem, and could help."

That gave me something to think about. A God so awesome that he could make even our stupid things turn out good. A God who cared for me that much.

That same afternoon, Hugh asked to have a word with me. I wasn't sure I wanted to talk to him, but couldn't think of an excuse not to. I found myself sitting opposite him at one of the red bistro tables, coffees in front of us. Hugh had a way of looking at you so that you had to look right back. He has really nice eyes, hazel and kind, sad sometimes but usually kind of twinkly. Mum told me that he'd lost his wife and child in a terrible accident.

"Annie," he said, "I'm sorry you've been a bit down in the dumps."

I bristled up a bit at that. Did Mum have to tell him *everything*? But he went on, "I just wanted you to know that I'd never, ever do anything to come between you and your mum. When a woman has children, they come first. Always." He rubbed his hand over his chin and his eyes were sad for a moment. I wondered if he was thinking of his own wife and child. Then he said, "I like your mum very much. We enjoy each other's company. I'd never do anything to hurt her." He was quiet for a moment and then said, "I'm thinking of asking her to the Alpha course at church. What do you think?"

I was rather astonished that he was asking my opinion. I'd been to the teen version of Alpha, a kind of group for people wanting to know more about Christianity, which Sadie and Rod had run at Beech Bank in the autumn. In fact, it was partly through them that I'd decided to ask Jesus into my life and become a Christian myself. I wasn't quite sure what Mum would make of it. But I was already warming to the idea. I said, "I think it would be cool."

Mum must have thought so too, because next Tuesday evening, the night they have the Alpha course, she was getting in quite a tizz about what to wear.

"What's the correct kind of thing to wear to church, Annie?" she asked, peering into the living room mirror. "I mean, is there a dress code?"

I looked at her, in black trousers and boots and a cream jumper. She looked nice. "Go just as you are, Mum. You look great."

She fluffed up her hair and looked anxious. "Should I wear a hat?"

I laughed. "Whatever for? It's in someone's house!

Why would you wear a hat?"

"I just thought people wore hats to church. My gran always did."

"Maybe they did in the olden days. Some of the really old ladies in the church wear a hat on Sundays. But then they wear hats all the time. There aren't any rules."

I thought how awful it would be if there were. Me and the girls wear whatever we want to; sometimes jeans, other times we get glammed up a bit for a special occasion. Some of the adults wear suits, others dress casual. It doesn't matter. Rod always welcomes everybody, even a smelly old tramp who comes in sometimes. He always says God looks on our hearts, not on our outward appearance.

My mother looked relieved. She went to do her face and put her coat on.

She didn't say much about the evening, except that it was interesting. But she went again the next week. And the next. By that time, I was feeling right back to my old self again. Snowdrops were out in all the gardens and birds were beginning to sing and chirp. The days were getting longer and the evenings lighter. Spring was coming.

The Alpha group was having a special weekend, where they went away together to a retreat place. I could see Mum liked the idea.

"It's a lovely old place, a kind of country mansion with beautiful grounds and amazing views," she said, showing me a picture of the place with daffodils in bloom.

"Why don't you go, Mum?" I said. "It would be a nice break."

"Oh, I couldn't," she said quickly. "What about you and Harry?"

I thought quickly. "Maybe Dad would have Harry, although it isn't his weekend. And I could stay with one of the girls."

She was dying to go, I could see. And suddenly I was determined that she would. I had a quick word with the girls next day.

"She's gotta go," said Rachel. "Come and stay at ours."

"Or ours," said Chloe. Like parrots, the rest all repeated the same two words. Of course, they'd need to consult their families. But I had a choice. How to decide.

In the end, I didn't go very far. Dad had a big business conference that weekend and couldn't have Harry after all. But Willow's family stepped in and said they'd have us both. They'd love to. They were still missing Granddad and it would be nice to have some company.

It was settled. We packed our bags, and round the corner to Willow's we went.

five

I like sleeping over at Willow's. I'd stayed a few times before, sometimes with one or two of the other girls, but it's always cool when it's just the two of us. Willow is more grown-up than the rest, even though she's the same age, and you can have sensible conversations with her. That's when Harry isn't there as well; when he and Rowan are together there's usually enough racket going on from their room to cause major distraction.

Harry sleeps on a little camp bed in Rowan's room. Willow's sleepover arrangements are more elaborate; a pale blue chair bed that has a really comfy sprung mattress and not just the pull-out foam affair that cheaper ones have. The only thing you have to watch out for are the metal supports underneath, which are just in the place you stand to get into the bed, and which I once stubbed my toe on very painfully.

Willow's house is very relaxed on the whole, although her dad is a teacher and lays down the law sometimes. Her mother, being an artist, is rather scatterbrained and doesn't go in much for being house-proud, so you have to clear up after yourself and sometimes get your own meals, too. Since Willow's granddad died, she's gone back to painting, and there were half-finished canvases stacked about and the smell of oil paints and cleaners. Willow likes the smell; she says it means everything's normal.

Willow's room is the complete opposite; all clean lines and immaculate furnishings, nothing left lying about. She's cut down a lot on the huge designer wardrobe she had, but the clothes she does have are always hung up in plastic covers or folded neatly, or put into the laundry basket if they need washing. She is an example to us all, as the rest of us are always being told by our mothers.

The first evening we stayed, Rowan and Harry were unusually rowdy, even for them. Thumps and shrieks kept coming from the next room. Willow and I were trying to catch up on our Chatspace friends, and having a hard job to concentrate. After a bit, she got up and banged on their door. "Rowan, cut it out!"

No answer, except for a few giggles and more thumps. Willow sighed and came back into our room. We were already in our PJs and had planned to get into our beds and have a nice chat with the lights out.

"I will personally strangle them in a minute," she muttered. I said I'd be pleased to help. We didn't have to, however, because shortly afterwards Willow's dad came up and read the riot act. Silence for a bit. We got into bed, switched off the light and settled down.

It was getting late and it wasn't long before we heard Willow's parents come up to bed. Shortly afterwards, some muffled shufflings and smothered laughter started up again from the boys' room. Willow sighed and switched the light back on. "None of us are going to get any sleep at this rate. Dad's going to go ballistic."

She got out of bed and went over to a battered old trunk under the window. I'd been wondering about it, because it stuck out like a sore thumb in Willow's tasteful room. It was obvious it had belonged to Willow's grandfather because it had his name on the side in black letters. Willow lifted the lid and rummaged about.

"What are you doing?"

"Looking for something. Ah, here it is." She pulled out what looked like a tatty old notebook, or part of one, with the cover gone and broken stitching showing at the back. She got back into bed with it.

"What's that?"

"Not really sure. Someone's old diary I found amongst Granddad's things. I think it must have been someone in our family because it's the same name. A girl our age, about a hundred years ago. I started reading it and just remembered it again now."

I was interested. "I wonder what it was like being young back then?"

Willow was turning the pages, taking care because they looked as though they might fall apart quite easily.

"I read a bit when I found it. She was called Grace and she lived on a farm. She had a brother and sister called Will and Carrie. I think parents were quite strict then and it sounds as though she didn't like some of the rules.

Ah, here we are."

I turned over towards her and propped my chin on my elbow. "Read a bit out loud."

Willow's hair stood out like a flame in the light of the bedside lamp. She frowned a bit in concentration and pulled a face at a loud thump from the boys' room. "OK. I'll start from where I left off before." She cleared her throat and began to read.

Aug 3rd

Will and Carrie and I went to band practice this evening. That is to say, he did, whilst we were at choir practice. Fortunately they are not held in the same building! I wore my new boots, which pinch a little as I am still breaking them in, but, let us be elegant or die, which is one of my Aunt Lily's sayings.

Aunt Lily is very stylish, you'd never guess that she and Mother are sisters. Mother does not altogether approve of her sister. Her opinion is that the place of girls and women is in the home, and that Aunt Lily should have a husband and family to care for, and not be gadding about the country putting her nose into men's affairs. She was scandalised when Aunt Lily joined the suffragette movement. And very perturbed when I said I admired her for it. Which I do. After all, the suffragettes succeeded in obtaining the vote for women, even though not until they are thirty and middle-aged. Well done them, say I! But I don't say it to Mother too often. I think she has a great fear that I may turn out like Aunt Lily.

*After choir, we went to the band hall to wait for Will
and were there when the band master had him play
his cornet solo. Will's playing has greatly improved.
When he stood playing his piece I felt shivers going
up and down my spine and my hair standing on end.
(Maybe that is an exaggeration.) And he has suddenly
grown very handsome too. He is tall and well-grown
for sixteen, and in his Sunday clothes with his hair
brushed he seems a different person than my big
brother. Carrie seemed quite bedazzled. I have a very
strong suspicion that she is sweet on Will.*

Willow lowered the book and glanced across at me.
"Carrie's not Grace and Will's sister, then. She must be
a friend."

I wanted to hear more. "Go on reading."

*On the way home, after we had left Carrie at her gate,
I thought I would test out Will's ideas about her, so
I said, "Do you think Carrie is pretty?" He kind of
frowned, as though his mind was on other things, and
then said, "Who, Carrots? I've never thought about it.
No, I wouldn't say so. Not with that carroty hair and
all those freckles. Not my idea of beauty."*

*I felt disappointed and rather cross with him.
Carrie is pretty, in her own way, and she detests being
called Carrots. And if he only knew how diligently she
applies buttermilk to her face to cure the freckles, he'd*

perhaps be less unkind. So I told him so, and he just
laughed and walked on ahead so fast I couldn't keep
up with him, whistling and swinging his cornet case.
Boys! Were there ever creatures more infuriating. I will
never be found mooning after any of them, however
handsome or musically talented. Although Archie
Humphreys and Tom Wainwright are rather nice-
looking too, and they blush when I look at them.

Willow paused for breath and grinned across at me.
"Grace seems like someone who knows her own mind. I
wish I'd met her."

I was getting hooked on Grace's journal now. "Read
some more?"

"OK."

"Thanks!"

Aug 5th

Suddenly, all the talk is of war. There have been
happenings on the continent of Europe, and it seems
that our country may be drawn in. Father says that
we must tend to our own affairs, we shall be busy with
harvest soon and that is more important than the
quarrels between nations. Mother does not like talk of
war. When I mentioned it to her she said I would be
better getting on with my work and listening less to
tittle-tattle. Now it's school holidays she keeps me busy.
After this summer, I will be starting at the Grammar
School, although I will have to be a boarder during

the week and I am not sure how I will like that. I am
excited but a little bit nervous . . .

So absorbed had we been in the diary that we hadn't
noticed doors opening and footfalls on the landing. Both
of us jumped as we heard Willow's dad's voice. Rowan
and Harry were getting a final warning. Next minute he
was tapping on our door too.

"Girls! That applies to you as well. It's getting late.
Lights out, please!"

He was using his sternest teacher's voice. Willow
pulled a face, said, "OK, Dad," put down the book and
switched off the light. Grace and her journal would have
to wait until another day.

PART THREE

Holly's Story

NEW ENTERPRISES

one

It was fun at first, having to live differently when my dad's business crashed. Well, maybe not fun exactly, but challenging. All of us had to think of ways to save money, and avoid spending it if possible. Our lovely house was on the market, but nobody seemed to want to buy it.

"These are very hard times," my dad kept reminding us. "The whole country is feeling the pinch. It's not just us."

So we still lived in our big house, and paid big bills, no matter how much we tried to cut down. Mum had found a part-time job in a local supermarket and I thought I should get one too, seeing as my pocket money had gone down to almost zilch.

The crunch came when I got a split in my winter boots. "I can actually feel the damp coming in," I complained.

"Oh dear, that's not good," said Mum, getting her worried look. "I thought they'd last you through the winter."

"There's a nice pair in Henderson's window," I said hopefully. "Black leather, perfect for school, and only £69.99 in the sale."

Mum looked at me with a helpless kind of expression. "Holly, that kind of money is way beyond us. I'm sorry. You have your wellies, and you'll have to manage with trainers for school."

I'd never had to manage with anything less than the best. I was beginning to dislike being poor.

"Do you know where I could get a job?" I asked at school lunchtime next day. Dad is handy and had managed to repair my boot, after a fashion. A patch inside. It was a bit uncomfortable but nobody could see it. It rubbed just enough to remind me I was wearing patched boots. Like something out of Oliver Twist. It didn't exactly inspire confidence.

Willow said, "There may be other people wanting somebody to do shopping or walk dogs, like I do Saturday mornings. I'll ask around if you like."

Most of the girls have Saturday jobs of one kind or another. Rachel helps out at the farm near her, taking care of retired horses and donkeys. Amber does sweeping up and taking towels to the laundrette for a local hairdresser. Chloe gets paid for doing housework by her Auntie Sue, who's a very particular kind of person. My mum used to be like that, but she doesn't have time these days, or the money to pay me to do it. Sigh. Annie's the only one who's OK for money, because she's got two lots of pocket money now her parents are divorcing. At least mine are staying together, which is something to be thankful for.

Annie sometimes finds it quite embarrassing, having money when the rest of us don't. "It doesn't seem

right. But I'll always lend you money if you need it. Or
. . ." I knew she was going to say she'd *give* us money,
but then didn't like to. It would be so humiliating to
have handouts from friends. I'd been in that privileged
position once, and I remembered how it was. Annie is
sensitive like that.

I gave her a hug. "You're the best. But I'll find some
way of earning money."

"There's always baby-sitting," said Rachel.

We did sometimes baby-sit at the vicarage for Josh
and Abi, who are cute kids but can sometimes be little
monsters and are hard work as well. I don't think I'd like
to do it too often.

"Rod and Sadie pay really well," said Chloe.

"Yes, but they're not asking us quite as much
nowadays," said Willow. "They get one of the grannies as
often as not. That's because they do it for free, I expect.
Rod and Sadie must be cutting down too. I don't think
vicars get paid that much."

We all sighed. "Still," said Rachel philosophically,
"we're well off by some standards. Think of Madalina
who came over from Romania last year – she was really
poor. And those African kids we saw on that mission
video. We're rich by comparison."

"Pity we couldn't go back to the barter system," said
Chloe. "You know, swapping cabbages for eggs, or digging
the baker's garden and getting free loaves of bread."

"Not much chance, with everything in supermarkets
these days," said Rachel.

We sighed again, finishing up the last of our apple crumble. Annie put down her spoon suddenly and made us all jump.

"I've had an idea!"

We all looked at her. "For a job for Holly?" asked Rachel.

"No, not exactly. But a kind of barter system we could do. A swap shop. I've heard of them in other places. People bring stuff they don't want and can take stuff they *do* want."

We chewed this over with the last of our pudding.

"It might work," said Willow cautiously. "But we'd need a place to keep the stuff."

"Beech Bank!" said Rachel and Amber together. "Let's ask Sadie."

Sadie seemed quite keen on the idea when we broached it to her later in the day.

"It could work," she said thoughtfully. "One man's trash is another man's treasure, as the saying goes. We could divide off a corner of the big hall, the space wouldn't be missed. Bring in a cupboard, maybe get Hugh to put up some shelves. Then we could put the stuff out at certain times. Maybe have it open to others now and again." She paused, thinking. "No money would be involved, so we wouldn't have bother with trading permissions or anything like that. There'd have to be rules. People only take something if they've brought something of roughly equal value."

"And no rubbish," said Willow. "It would have to be

good quality."

"And in good condition. No old tat."

"Er – but wouldn't it be embarrassing, wearing something we'd seen on some one else?"

"Not necessarily. It wouldn't be just clothes. We could have sports stuff, footballs and tennis rackets. Phones, some people are always getting new ones. Computer games. Household stuff."

"Oooh, we could bring all the Christmas pressies we don't like. I had loads of toiletries and stuff I'll never use, all brand new in boxes. And Mum had heaps of stuff she'll never use."

I was beginning to feel quite keen on this idea. I had loads of stuff from younger days I didn't need any more. We were all getting quite carried away.

"Books!" said Chloe. "People could even read them and bring them back, like a library. And kids' clothes. Lampshades! Pictures!"

"Whoa," said Sadie, laughing. "Hold your horses! Remember we won't have unlimited space. I think we'll have to say that if something isn't taken after a month, the donor takes it back. But I think it's a good idea. It could be a real help to the community."

And that's how it all happened. Rod approved of the idea too, and so did Hugh, and so did our parents. The Beech Bank Swap Shop was born.

two

It all got going quite quickly once the idea caught on. Hugh put in a storage cabinet and a shelf unit and a folding table. We made a big poster to go on the wall "BEECH BANK SWAP SHOP", and some notices for the front of the building explaining what it was all about. Rod put up extra ones on the church notice board and in public places like the Post Office and the supermarket. In no time, the stuff came flooding in.

Trouble was, despite the notices, some folk seemed to misunderstand what it was all about. A lady turned up one afternoon with two bulging bin bags of clothing.

"For your jumble sale. I've been having a clear out."

The last thing we wanted was a pile of discarded clothing. Sadie explained as tactfully as she could, showing the lady the notice on the front door.

"People bring in just one item. And then take one away. We only have limited space, you see. It was a kind thought, but it's not a jumble sale."

The lady was rather sniffy with us. "Oh, I see. I thought you'd be glad of them. Just have to take them to the clothing bins in the car park then. I wish I'd known."

She went off, a bin bag in each hand. Sadie sighed. We were all beginning to wonder if we'd bitten off more than we could chew.

Things settled after a bit, when people got the hang of what we were doing. Some really nice things were donated. A beautiful Barbie house, with furniture all complete and pristine. The parent who brought it in took away a brand-new set of make-up in a pretty case. Her little girl had grown up. Amber's mum took the Barbie house for Lucy, and donated a brand-new dog bed that their dog refused to sleep in. Someone took the dog bed and brought a pretty bedside lamp. Business was booming.

The Swap Shop was only open for an hour on Friday afternoons, when other people were allowed in, too. We girls were kept busy setting things out, dealing with people who wanted help or advice, tidying and putting things away. Some good swaps came our way too. Chloe brought in a complete set of teenage novels and took away a set of encyclopaedias.

"Only you would want encyclopaedias," said Amber, searching round for a box for Chloe to carry them home in.

"Yes, well, they're amazing. Full of interesting stuff. I've grown out of that teenage girl stuff anyway. Bor – ing!"

I got a real bargain too. I donated a very expensive pair of sunglasses I'd had for our visit to Australia, before Dad's business crashed.

"Why don't you keep them," said Mum. "It might be a

long time before we can afford anything like that again."

"It'll be a long time before we have another sunshine holiday," I said, and then felt mean when Mum's face clouded over. "I've got another pair, Mum. I don't need these."

I got a real bargain in return, in my opinion. Not boots, but a big, brown, genuine leather bag, with a shoulder strap and pockets and buckles and best of all, a designer label. It was well worn and a bit scuffed but that was partly why I liked it. In fact, I loved it, and the others were well envious, but I'd spotted it first. I slung it over my shoulder to go home.

"This is going to be my school bag," I told Mum. She was a bit critical, and I could see she thought I'd have been better off keeping my designer shades.

"It's rather scruffy looking," she said. "The corners are quite worn."

"The worn-leather vintage look is in at the moment," I told her. "Quality that's stood the test of time."

"Well, if you put it like that . . ."

Upstairs, I investigated the many pockets and zipped compartments. One would do nicely for my phone. Another for my purse. I unzipped that one and caught my breath. There was a small purse already there. Not one that matched the bag either, it was black leather and not brown. I undid the clasp and caught my breath again. There was money in the purse, ten-pound notes folded flat. I took them out and counted – ten, twenty, thirty, forty – right up to ninety pounds.

And a fiver. Ninety five pounds.

I sat on the bed and rummaged through the purse and the bag, looking for some evidence of who it had belonged to. I'd no idea who had brought it in. So many people had been in and out. The purse had obviously been left in the bag by mistake.

Then I stopped rummaging, struck by a thought. The bag had been donated, purse and all. Wouldn't that mean that whoever got to take the bag was entitled to the contents too? Including the purse and money? Ninety five pounds! I could buy a nice pair of boots with that and have cash to spare.

I sat there for a moment, trying to think clearly. I remembered a shopping trip with the girls last year, when we'd been in Chadwick's trying on clothes. Annie had left her purse in the changing cubicle, and Willow had gone in next and been tempted to take some money for something she really wanted. She didn't though, and she even confessed to us what had been in her mind.

This was different though, surely. It wouldn't be stealing. Would it? I'd swapped in all good faith. It wasn't my fault. No one would know.

God would. That thought came clearly, cutting through the others. That money wasn't mine. It would be as good as stealing, it would be dishonest, and dishonesty was forbidden by God. I belonged to him, ever since I'd asked Jesus into my heart and life, and I wanted to obey him.

I couldn't do it.

I sighed, and picked up the purse again. I didn't even

have to ask Mum and Dad or Sadie and Rod for advice, because I knew what they'd say. The purse must be returned. But how could I do that when I didn't know who it belonged to?

A checkout receipt was in one of the purse compartments, an old one and a bit faded. It didn't tell me much except that the person had bought potatoes, carrots, bread, milk, dog food and all the usual stuff. The date was illegible. And then – bingo! My searching fingers found something else, a small card, the kind people give out with all their details, and it was all here, a name, address, phone number. And it looked clean and new, not dog-eared and out of date. The address was here, in our town, though I didn't recognise the area. "Susan J. Dalrymple, 6 Riverside Gardens".

three

"Riverside Gardens?" said Amber. "That's those new houses, isn't it, over the other side of town. Not far from Willow's and Annie's?"

I'd been wondering whether I should phone Susan J. Dalrymple, or just turn up with the purse. I thought the latter might be less trouble in the long run. I decided to go right after school next day, before Beech Bank.

"I'll go with you," said Willow. "It's practically round the corner from me."

"Me too," said Annie. "For moral support."

I knew they also wanted to come so they could have a bit of a nose round. Riverside Gardens is rather posh, it seems, and they were itching to see Susan J. Dalrymple, someone apparently so rich that she casually gave away bags with almost a hundred pounds in them. The others would have liked to come too, but they live right the other end of town, and besides, it might have looked very odd if a whole bunch of us turned up. I promised to give them a full report.

As it was, I was nervous enough when we turned into the entrance to Riverside Gardens. Our house is lovely, but these were something else, kind of Swiss-looking, like the chalets we stay in on skiing holidays (correction, the ones we *used* to stay in when we *had* skiing holidays). One storey buildings with peaked roofs, wrap-around decks and picture-windows overlooking the river. They must have cost a bomb. I wondered however people could afford them these days.

"Only six of them," said Annie. "Very exclusive."

"All that beautiful wood!" said Willow. "I so love wooden houses. That's the kind I'm going to live in."

"You and Jay, of course," said Annie slyly.

"Oh, shut up!" said Willow.

We were walking up to the front door of number 6, and I had butterflies. The gardens weren't finished yet, but you could see they were going to be beautifully landscaped too. I rang the front doorbell.

It seemed a long time before it was answered. The door was opened by an elderly lady, not at all the kind of person I'd expect to live in a house like that. She looked like a typical countrywoman: tweed skirt, woolly cardigan, thick stockings and sensible shoes. She had grey hair cut short and carried a chunky walking stick. Somewhere in the back of the house, a dog barked.

"Yes?" she said, peering at us. "Can I help you? If you are collecting for something, I shall want to know exactly how the money is to be used, with written documentation. Otherwise I will not consider donating."

"Er – we're not collecting," I said nervously. "In fact, we have something that we think is yours. Er – are you Miss Dalrymple?"

"Mrs. Well, what is it?"

I fished about in my school bag. I hadn't yet transferred my stuff to the brown leather one. I pulled out the purse and held it out to her.

"This was in the bag that was donated to the Beech Bank Swap Shop." I was glad to notice that my voice was sounding less quivery now. "There's money inside."

Mrs. Dalrymple seemed quite gobsmacked. She said, "Good gracious!" and took the purse. She opened it and leafed through the notes, and said, "Good gracious!" again. Then she looked at us and said, "Please come in."

We hadn't intended on visiting, but it seemed impolite to refuse. Besides, I knew we'd all like a look at the inside of the house. We trooped in.

The end of the hallway was all glass, overlooking the river. There was a lovely smell inside, of sawn wood and fresh plaster. Everything was new. Timber beams soared up to the rafters in the apex. Mrs. Dalrymple led us into a big airy living-room, also with a spectacular view of the river and the trees fringing the opposite bank. The three of us sat in a row on one of those sofas with ends that let down.

"Would you like something to drink?" asked Mrs. Dalrymple, leaning on her stick. I noticed that her hands looked all knotted and bumpy. "I expect you'd like lemonade. I had a Guide troop of girls your age and they loved their lemonade. I'm afraid I don't have any, but I could make you a cup of tea?"

We declined the tea by common consent. At the rate Mrs. Dalrymple moved, it would take half the evening to make it. She sat down opposite in a high wing chair, clutching her stick in front of her. "Well now, I am very grateful to you for returning the purse. It is quite refreshing to find that there are still honest young people in the world."

"It was Holly, really," said Willow. "She got the bag from our Swap Shop at Beech Bank."

Mrs. Dalrymple looked at me out of faded blue eyes. "Thank you so much, Hayley. I thought that purse and money had gone for good. I was afraid it had been lost in the move. Clara – my daughter – insisted on taking a great many of my things to the charity shops. She mentioned that the bag had gone to a church sale or something. I had no idea the purse was inside." She sighed. "So many things had to go. I needed to downsize, you see."

We glanced sideways at each other. If this was downsizing, whatever kind of place had she lived in before? As though she could read our thoughts, she said, "I've been at Barrington Court all my married life, almost fifty years. I couldn't bear to leave, even after my husband died. I kept it on as long as I could, but, my arthritis has worsened – and the old place was draughty and a bit damp, which didn't help. And of course, it's so difficult to find reliable staff these days. Clara lives in New Zealand, but she came over for six months, found this place for me and moved me in." She sighed again. "She left just two days ago. And here we are, just the two of us now. Just Barkis and me."

We exchanged sideways looks again, wondering who Barkis could be. The name seemed familiar, and I remembered where I'd heard it – from *David Copperfield*, which we did in English last year. Barkis was a cabbie, I recalled, quite keen on Peggoty, and when he wanted to propose, he sent a message saying "Barkis is willing." Did Mrs. Dalrymple have a butler or something called Barkis?

"That's him you can hear in the background," said Mrs. Dalrymple.

All the time we'd been talking, the dog had not stopped barking from another room, not the furious crescendo kind of barking that dogs do when people invade their territory, but a monotonous, deep, constant bark, bark,

bark. He certainly had the right name. I felt Annie give a smothered giggle, and I was having difficulty keeping a straight face. Willow dug me in the ribs.

"He'll keep it up for hours on end, poor old fellow," said Mrs. Dalrymple. "Boredom, mostly. I let him out for a run in the garden morning and evening, but I can't walk him any more." She peered at us. "I don't suppose you know anyone who does dog walking? I'd pay well."

I looked at Willow. She does dog walking on Saturdays for one or two people. This wasn't far from her house and might fit in perfectly. I expected her to say she'd do it. But instead, she looked right back at me, took a deep breath, and said, "Yes. Holly does."

four

Mrs. Dalrymple peered at me. "Well, that's a stroke of good fortune! Would you consider taking on Barkis? As often as you could – every day, if possible. I'd pay well. Say ten pounds a time?"

I gulped, not knowing how to reply. Ten pounds a day, that would be seventy pounds a week, if I did it every day! I'd have my boots within a week! We've never had a dog at home, and the only one I know well is Amber's dog, Hamlet, who's a bit of a clown. But there's no big deal to dog-walking, surely. Just a matter of holding the end of a lead and walking. An easy way of earning money. Willow nudged me again, and I heard myself saying, "Oh, well – yes. Yes, thank you. I'll do it."

Mrs. Dalrymple beamed. "Thank you so much. I know you're an honest girl, because you returned my purse so promptly. Would you like to meet Barkis?"

Well, we couldn't very well say no. Mrs. Dalrymple hobbled to a door off the hallway. The barking stopped and we heard her speaking to the dog. Then they both came back to the living room.

Barkis turned out to be a basset hound, a strange-looking animal who seemed as slow and elderly as his owner. He had a long, stretched-out kind of body, very short legs, long drooping ears and a mournful expression. He looked sadly at us, then came and sniffed carefully at each of us in turn, his nose twitching frantically.

"He's very lovable," said Mrs. Dalrymple fondly, sitting down again. "Completely untrainable, of course – bassets are a law unto themselves and can't even be house-trained. That's why he has to remain in the laundry room for such long spells. They're hounds, you see. Following a scent is what they love. In his younger days, Barkis would follow an exciting scent for hours. He once took a fancy to a group of hikers on a footpath across our land, and we had to retrieve him from a Youth Hostel nine miles away."

At the moment, Barkis was finding the smell of my patched boots very interesting.

"He likes you, Hilly," declared Mrs. Dalrymple. "Give him a stroke. Get to know him. He's very affectionate."

I gingerly gave Barkis a pat on his domed head. He looked up at me with the same mournful expression, but his tail began to wag furiously.

"There! He's taken to you!" said Mrs. Dalrymple triumphantly. "I can see you'll get along wonderfully well. Will about this time tomorrow suit you? Oh, and here's a little something in advance, and as a reward for your honesty."

The little something turned out to be two ten pound notes from the ones in the purse.

I was a little breathless by the time we left Riverside Gardens and headed for Beech Bank. Willow and Annie were gleeful.

"You're quids in there, Holls!"

"Money for old rope!"

"It's true what they say. Honesty is the best policy."

I had to admit that I seemed to have fallen on my feet. We'd missed half an hour of BB time, but hey, as Willow said, I just needed to keep the ten-pound signs flashing in front of my eyes. God had really come through for me this time.

I turned up right after school next day for my first walk with Barkis. He was all ready to go, tail waving and looking a lot brighter, as though he knew the days were over when he had to stay hopelessly barking in the laundry room.

"Thirty minutes or so will be enough," Mrs. Dalrymple

told me. "Barkis is not young any more, like me. Also, Bassetts don't have strong hearts. It's the breeding, you see – they're bred to an unnatural shape which puts strain on the organs."

I couldn't argue that Barkis' shape was a little unusual. We set off along the river bank. Barkis didn't exactly walk, it was more of a waddle. And not a brisk one either. Now that he was out, Barkis felt he had to investigate every tuft of grass, every tree trunk, every rabbit hole and root and stone. He had to stop and sniff and sniff, determining whether other dogs had passed that way. Then he had to leave his own mark. If I encouraged him to move on he ignored me. If I tried to pull on the lead, he simply dug his toes in until he was good and ready. Bassets may not have strong hearts, but they sure have powerful shoulders, plus a very stubborn streak.

We reached the lane leading up into town, and I thought we'd go back that way and avoid the trees and bushes and other interesting scents along the bank. Bad idea. There were plenty of lampposts, street corners, gateways and parked cars, all of which Barkis had to stop and examine and sniff, and leave his mark. And there were people too, which made for a lot of embarrassment on my part. I'd stick to the river bank next time, I decided.

But it was worth it to see the gratitude on Mrs. Dalrymple's face.

"Oh, he looks so much brighter! Did you have nice walkies, darling?"

Barkis flopped down on the hearthrug, tired and

content. The walking had been a success, from his point of view at any rate.

So my new routine was established, taking Barkis out right after school each day before going to Beech Bank. Mum and Dad were a little dubious to begin with about my new employment, though.

"We don't know this person at all," said Mum, who can be very worrisome at times.

"Mum, she's an old lady on her own, with such bad arthritis she can hardly walk, not an axe murderer or something."

"All the same, we should have met her first. Maybe Dad will go with you tomorrow."

I groaned. I didn't want Mrs. Dalrymple checked out. I was beginning to like her a lot. But Dad met me from school next day and drove me to Riverside Gardens. Being a builder by trade himself, the construction of the buildings interested him very much, and he was inclined to poke around and look at everything. When I introduced him to Mrs. D. she immediately latched on to the information that he'd been a builder.

"There's a storage cupboard in the cloakroom that doesn't work for me. I just cannot reach the high shelves. Could something be done? And some of the doors seem to be stiff. Could you look at them?"

Barkis and I left them to it and set off on our walk. When we got back, Dad was still there, having a cup of tea with Mrs. D. He'd already agreed to adjust the shelves, fix the doors, check out an inconvenient bathroom fitting and maybe construct a greenhouse. He'd been obliged to go on benefits since his business crashed, but was allowed to work a certain number of hours each week. It would fit in nicely, and be very helpful all round. He was in an excellent mood as he dropped me off at Beech Bank and I breathed a sigh of relief. Mum would get a positive report, and I'd get the thumbs-up for the job.

five

I wasn't too keen on walks with Barkis the first few times, but after a while I found I was actually enjoying them. All those stops and waits meant that I could really look at the scenery and the plants and things growing along the river bank, which I'd never done before. I noticed the bright yellow celandines, as shiny as though they'd been lacquered, the delicate pale yellow of the first primroses, powdery catkins and fluffy pussy-willow blossoms. I saw how the river itself changed and looked different in different weather and different lights. I watched buds on trees bursting out a little more every day. Mrs. Dalrymple gave me a little book on wild flowers and plants, which I could carry in my pocket and identify things I didn't know.

I soon got fond of Mrs. Dalrymple, too. She was a kind-hearted lady, a bit absent-minded but very lovable, like her dog. Once she'd got the hang of my name, and stopped calling me Hayley or Hilly, or Molly or Polly or Dolly, we got along like a house on fire. When Saturday came, I didn't wait until the usual after-school time, but went round right after lunch.

Going up the path to number 6, I had an idea. "Is there anything else I could do for you, Mrs. Dalrymple?" I asked, as Barkis gave me his usual greeting of sniffing my feet and legs while his tail waved furiously. "Some shopping at the Co-op? Housework? Or tidying up in the garden? I wouldn't charge any more, of course."

She smiled at me. "That's kind, dear. You're a very kind girl. But I get all my shopping delivered to the door. I have a cleaner three times a week. As for the garden, well, after the landscape people have done their work I'll be hiring someone to keep it up."

Of course. Whatever Mrs. D.'s disadvantages, lack of money wasn't one of them.

After I'd delivered Barkis safely home, I decided to swing round by Annie's and Willow's and maybe hang out for a while with one, or both, of them. As I approached Annie's house, she opened the door and came out.

"Hey!" she said. "Have you been doing the Dreaded Dog Duties?"

I laughed. "I'm getting to like it. You off somewhere?"

"Only to Willow's. She's got some diary thing she started to read to me when I slept over. I was a bit bored so I just texted her and asked if I could hear some more. Why don't you come?"

She linked her arm in mine. Walking along, I said thoughtfully, "You know what, I'm really glad I picked up that old bag."

Annie looked a bit surprised and then burst out laughing. "Thought you meant Mrs. D. there for a moment."

That really cracked me up too. When I'd got my breath again, I said, "I'm so glad I didn't keep the money. I thought about it, I really did. I could have spent it in dribs and drabs, a bit at a time. Nobody would have known."

Annie became serious too. "*You'd* have known. And you'd have got all stressed out feeling guilty and covering up. It would always have been on your mind. You wouldn't have enjoyed spending it."

I nodded. "Yeah. And if my mum and dad had ever found out, they'd have been well ashamed. Disappointed in me, big time. You know what they're like. As it is, I've got a fab job I like, I'll soon have loads of dosh, and Dad has got some work with Mrs. D. as well. How great is that?"

We high-fived each other. Walking on, Annie said thoughtfully, "I guess it's always better to do things the right way. God's way."

I'd been doing some thinking too. I knew Annie wouldn't laugh at me, so I told her what was on my mind. "You know what? I'm not even sure I want to spend all the money on myself."

Annie looked surprised. "Not even on new boots?"

"Well, maybe. But I don't mind these old patched ones so much any more. I reckon they have a kind of cool, vintage look. Winter will soon be over anyway. And I'm thinking I'll give a bit to Mum towards housekeeping every week. And put some towards our gap year mission project."

Annie didn't say any more, but she gave my arm a quick squeeze.

At Willow's, her mum answered the door in a paint-smeared smock. "Hello girls. Willow's up in her room. Go on up."

We picked our way up the stairs, cluttered as they always were with books, trainers, and the odd jar full of paintbrushes. Going into Willow's room is always like entering some cool, serene oasis of order and peace. She was lying on her tummy on the bed, propped up on her elbows, reading a tatty-looking old exercise book. She was pleased to see us.

"Hi guys! Make yourselves at home. This stuff is well cool. Do you want to hear some?"

We settled ourselves, Annie on the chair bed, me on the beanbag. Willow did a quick recap for my benefit. "This is the diary of a fourteen-year-old girl, Grace. It starts in 1914 but I think it goes on longer. I've got to where war has just been declared – the First World War, you know – and all the guys are joining up. I'll just carry on from where I've got to."

We made ourselves comfortable, and Willow began.

Aug 12th

It's as though we are in the grip of war-fever. Everyone
talks about nothing else these days. The whole world
has gone topsy-turvy. All we hear is the war effort,
and what can be done to support our brave boys.
Everywhere you look there are posters of that man,
Lord Kitchener, pointing his finger and saying "Your
country needs YOU!" Not that the lads need much
persuasion. Even here, they are enlisting as fast as they
can, just longing to get into that khaki uniform and get
the training done and be off to serve King and country.
Archie Humphreys and Tom Wainwright have enlisted
already, you should see them swaggering about and
boasting. Mother says she thanks God Will is not old
enough for the services.

Aug 16th

A big parade today. All the local lads who have joined
the army along with others from the villages and farms
around, marched through the town in their uniforms
and with their weapons. Our brass band went in
front, playing rousing songs like "It's a long way to
Tipperary" and "Goodbye Dolly". It seemed everyone
for miles around had turned out to line the streets and
there was quite a crush. Everyone was cheering them
on and all the little children had Union Jacks to wave.
We kept seeing faces of lads we knew, familiar, but very
different as well under their helmets. They all looked so
proud, already they are heroes.

Aug 17th

Yesterday's parade ended in a distressing way. During the parade, I noticed an odd thing. Some of the girls were giving out flowers to the brave soldiers, throwing them or running out among the khaki uniforms. Then I saw that one girl, a stranger to me so someone visiting for the occasion, run among the bandsmen and pressed something into our Will's hand. I thought it must be a flower too, he looked as strong and handsome as any of the soldier boys. I know Carrie thought so!

Will walked home with us as usual, and his face was like thunder. Carrie and I didn't know what to make of it, so did not ask. But when we'd left Carrie, my curiosity got the better of me, and I said "Will, what is the matter? Didn't you enjoy the parade?"

He shook his head and I saw his fists clench. Then I remembered the girl who had put something into his hand. I was going to ask, but I did not need to, for he turned to me with such a fierce look and said in a strange voice, "I am shamed and made a spectacle. Look what was put into my hand." He took his hand from his pocket and showed me, with his eyes full of hurt and shame. It was a crumpled white feather.

Willow paused and looked across at us. I found I'd been holding my breath, and Annie's face was rapt. "Do you know what that means?" asked Willow. We didn't. Annie was just asking her to read on, when there was a bleep on my phone to say someone had texted. I was going to ignore it, but saw it was from Mum, at work.

"I'm doing an extra hour. Could you pick up 500g of lean mince from the butcher and make a start on the chilli?"

I checked the time and groaned. The butcher's would be closed if I didn't get a move on. I'd have to rush.

"Willow," I said, "please can we come round again soon and read some more? I can't wait to find out what happens next!"

PART FOUR

Amber's Story

BIG MISTAKES

one

"Isn't it a shame," I said thoughtfully, stirring my coffee, "that the boys round here are all so – depressing."

Chloe looked a bit surprised, but then she nodded. "Yeah. I see what you mean, now that you mention it."

Both of us looked across at the open doorway to the games area, where several of the boys who go to Beech Bank were shooting pool. Nearly all of them were still in their school uniform, which meant black trousers, crumpled shirts half tucked in and half hanging out, and ties either pulled loose and skew-whiff, or stuffed into their pockets. Most of them had gelled hair, some had spots, one had a brace on his teeth and all of them were showing off and trying to pretend they were The Man. Now and again you'd catch one of them looking sideways at us girls, though they always pretended they weren't if they saw we'd noticed. Very juvenile behaviour, in my opinion.

"They're OK really," said Chloe, "but the thing is they're all so *young*. Most of them are from our year at school." She sighed. "Well, it's a good thing I'm not looking for a boyfriend at the moment."

I looked at her. Blonde, slim and drop-dead gorgeous. I knew that half the boys in our year fancied her like mad. Trouble is, she's such a bookish person and the guys are too scared of her to ask her out. I'd always thought she wasn't that interested but maybe I'd been wrong. She's very choosy though, and it would take a really top guy to impress her.

Just at that moment, the pool ball shot right off the table and rolled across the floor towards our wrought-iron bistro table. Chloe picked it up and held it out in the palm of her hand. Ben Freeman came over and took it, red as a beetroot, mumbled thanks without meeting her eyes, and almost tripped over his feet as he turned back to the pool table. I know he's one that fancies her.

"Dope," I said. "See what I mean?"

"He's just shy," said Chloe.

I sighed. In my opinion, none of the lads here were at all appealing, and neither were the ones at school. OK for shooting a game of pool with, or having a joke with, like I do with my brothers, but not exactly boyfriend material. Not that any of them took much notice of me anyway, brown-haired, average and unremarkable as I am, especially when Chloe's about. I took a sip of my coffee.

"It'll be a miracle if we ever get half-way decent boyfriends, if you ask me," I said moodily.

"Sadie would say that God will bring them along when the time is right," said Chloe. "Like with Willow and Jay."

"And Willow wasn't even looking," I said. "It just

happened. Their eyes met across a crowded room and wham, that was it. Love at first sight."

"Not that Willow ever admits it," said Chloe. "She's always insisting they're just good friends. A case of 'methinks she doth protest too much' if you ask me. But have you noticed the way she kind of lights up when he phones or texts, or when she's just thinking about him?"

I'd noticed. And been a bit envious, to be honest. Jay's about eighteen, fit, tall, tanned and a lovely guy as well. He has it all. I sighed.

"I can't see anything like that ever happening to me. I'd love someone in my life who made me feel like that."

"Tell you what," said Chloe, "let's make a list of all the things we'd like in an ideal boyfriend."

It seemed as good a way as any to fill in the time while we waited for the others to finish their homework. Chloe rummaged in her bag and pulled out a notebook and a couple of pens. She pushed a piece of paper over to me. "Here. List five attributes for the perfect boyfriend."

We scribbled and thought hard for a few minutes.

"Now let's share our ideas," said Chloe.

Her list read:

1. Intelligent
2. Reads books
3. Sense of humour
4. Kind
5. Reasonably good looking

Mine read:

1. Gawjuss looking
2. Absolutely no acne, spots, zits etc
3. No bad habits, like nose picking, looking in every mirror he passes etc
4. Likes animals
5. Someone with a motor-bike would be a bonus

I had to admit mine sounded rather immature, negative and a bit silly, compared with hers.

"What about Christian beliefs, though?" said Chloe. "Neither of us mentioned that."

I had noticed. It should have been top of the list, I supposed. I sighed again. Sometimes it's hard to be cool *and* a Christian.

"Talking of motorbikes," said Chloe. "Have you noticed those ones that gather at the top of the car park now the evenings are lighter? Quite a lot of them."

I had noticed them in passing, mostly if I was in the car. When Chloe and Holly and I go home from BB, we take a short cut through the town that doesn't go by the main car park. Chloe and I looked at each other. "We *could* do a little detour and go home that way," I said thoughtfully. "Especially as Holly's not here today. What do you think?"

"You mean, to check out the guys? Or the bikes?"

"Well, maybe both. I'm interested in bikes. And it's where the guys a bit older hang out. I'm not suggesting we go and *talk* to them, or anything like that. We'd just be walking past that way on our way home."

Chloe looked doubtful. "Auntie Sue would have a fit if she thought I was parading about in front of boys. Especially bikers."

"Well, maybe my mum would too. But we wouldn't be *parading*. Just walking home. No harm in that. And it's still broad daylight after club now."

I could see she was still not quite convinced. But I was sure she'd see my point. Those lads were mostly about sixteen plus. There might be some cool dudes among them. And let's face it, we hadn't much chance of meeting boys any other way. Our social life is not exactly sparkling.

Willow, Rachel and Annie were emerging from the homework area and heading our way. I had the feeling they wouldn't exactly approve of the way our conversation had been heading. I could see Chloe thought so too. By tacit agreement we put the subject on hold for another time, and began discussing the latest daft thing my dog Hamlet had done.

two

We didn't go home by way of the car park that evening, because Holly turned up after all, late from her dog walking, so naturally we all walked home together. For some reason we didn't want Holly to be with us. For one thing, she's confident when it comes to boys. Being an only child, she's been with adults a lot, and used to going to social events with her parents. She can converse intelligently on most subjects, doesn't blush easily and seems to fall on her feet after any disaster. She's also stunning to look at. Chloe and I feel quite handicapped by the side of her, Chloe with her shyness and me with my plainness. The last thing we wanted was for Holly to think we had "desperate" invisibly tattooed on our foreheads when it came to boys.

But the following afternoon Holly had an appointment with the orthodontist, and Chloe and I found ourselves taking the long route home. The biker lads were there; we could hear the revving of engines before we reached the car park. There was quite a bunch of them, five or six in leathers and bomber jackets, others in ordinary clothes looking at the bikes. Even a couple of girls. They were just hanging out, sitting on the bikes, or looking at the engines, or discussing their performance.

I quite like bikes; both my big brothers had them for a while, until Charlie swapped his for a car and Sam sold his to help pay student expenses, much to my mum's relief. She'd never let me go on the back, though I did sneak a ride once or twice when she wasn't about. I loved the feeling of controlled power, the smell of exhaust fumes and the feel of wind on my face.

"Nice bikes," I said to Chloe as we drew level.

Chloe kept her head down and didn't even look at them. "I don't like them. Nasty noisy, dangerous things."

The group of lads had noticed us though, or at least, they'd noticed Chloe. Probably I hadn't even registered. One of them called out "Hey, Blondie!" and another one whistled. Chloe completely ignored them, just kept walking and never even turned her head. I sneaked a sideways look and saw a couple of them grinning. Some had helmets on, others hadn't, and I noticed one lad with dark curly hair and very white teeth showing in a big grin. The girls with them were giving us hard looks.

A minute or two later, we'd turned the corner, and a minute after that, the bikes roared into life and passed us by, heading out towards the countryside. One or two of them hooted and hollered as they passed us. I looked after them rather wistfully. I'd love to have been on one of those pillions, heading out to the wide blue yonder.

Chloe was not impressed. "A bit moronic, if you ask

me. Showing off and polluting the atmosphere."

"Oh, I don't know. They looked OK. Some of them are in the sixth form, I think."

"Well, we've done the car park route and checked out the bikers. Think we'll stick to the usual one in future."

I was disappointed. I'd have liked a bit of follow-up.

Next morning, Saturday, I was up in good time to take Hamlet for a walk before I did my Saturday morning job at the salon. It was a lovely morning, birds warbling away and sun shining. Back home, I kicked off my wellies and went upstairs to get ready. I'm supposed to create a good impression, even if I'm just the Saturday girl, and I have to wear black trousers and a white top.

I had a good look at myself in the bathroom mirror, wondering if I should get a new haircut or even a new colour. Bev, my boss at the salon, would give me discount rates. But what style? What colour? I looked at my eyes, kind of greenish. Hair: brownish. Skin: not bad. No spots anyway, I hate spots. Nose: medium. Mouth: a fraction too wide. Teeth: good, thanks to Mum insisting on me keeping all my dentists' and hygienists' appointments.

I sighed (I seemed to be doing a lot of sighing lately), and thought of one word descriptions of me and my mates. Holly: stunning. Chloe: beautiful. Willow: striking. Annie: appealing. Rachel: doe-like (because of her beautiful eyes). Me: nondescript.

"Amber!" yelled Mum up the stairs. "You're going to be late!"

It was a bit quiet at the salon that morning, and I

plucked up the courage to consult Bev about hairstyles. Bev is one of those larger-than-life people, all boobs and false eyelashes and heart as big as a bucket. The clients love her, and pour out all their troubles into her ears.

"A new style?" she said, taking me by the shoulders and holding me at arm's length. "I know just the perfect one for you." She consulted her watch. "And I have nobody for half an hour. I'll do you right now. Pop an overall on."

And before I knew it, I was sitting in a swivel chair with Bev snipping and scissoring and turning my head this way and that. Eventually she said, "There! Take a good look."

I lifted my head and said, "Wow!" Bev was a genius! She'd transformed my longish, ordinary head of hair into a neat, sleek bob, parted at one side and dipping attractively over at the other.

"Special occasion this evening?" she asked, and without waiting for a reply, went on, "I'll just put on a spray of this to give an extra shine." Wow again! If only there was a special occasion . . .

A load of towels was almost ready to take to the laundrette. "You have ten minutes to spare," said Bev. "While you're waiting, why don't you pop up to the bathroom and put on a bit of make-up. Here, try this lipstick. Goes with your colouring."

She produced a brand-new tube and pressed it into my hand. "New look to go with new hairdo."

I don't normally go for a lot of make-up, but I was

amazed at what a difference a bit of eyeliner, mascara and the new lipstick made. A different girl stared back at me from the mirror. Bev was a miracle-worker! She clearly thought so too, when I went back to the salon. "Woo hoo! The face of the decade! Keep the lipstick! OK, off you go with the towels, and practice holding your head up high and strutting your stuff!"

I did feel different, despite the fact that I was towing a trolley full of damp towels. Several people looked twice at me, and one lady I knew from church passed by without recognising me. Amazing what a makeover can do for confidence levels.

The laundrette was fairly quiet and I didn't have to wait for a machine. There were just two other people; a large lady and a young guy. The large lady left just as I finished loading the last pink towel. I went to fetch conditioner and noticed that the young guy was throwing several pairs of jeans into his machine. I had a fleeting thought that maybe he was going to strip down to his underwear, like the lad in the famous TV advert. But he didn't, he just tossed in the last pair and turned to face me. I almost fainted on the spot. I recognised the dark curly hair and the teeth. The biker from the car park.

three

All my mates call me the Drama Queen, and I must admit I do like a bit of dramatic input in my life. My dad calls me a prima donna, which he thinks means someone who likes to be the centre of attention. Not sure he's got it quite right, but there's some truth in it, maybe.

In a situation like this, it should have been a matter of looking deep into his dark, mysterious eyes, him looking into mine, and a sense of recognition flashing like electricity between us. He'd have said something like, "So you're the person I've been waiting for all my life," and I would acknowledge the fact with a sweet smile and a demure lowering of my long-lashed eyelids.

The reality was a little more down to earth. He simply glanced at me and said, "Have you finished with the conditioner?" and when I mumbled, "Er – yes," he said, "Ta."

But when both our machines had whirred into life, he turned to face me again. I made a big thing of wheeling my trolley to the side and parking it out of the way.

"Do I know you from somewhere?" he asked. I looked up, really glad I'd let Bev work on me that morning. But in spite of the makeover, I couldn't think of anything more scintillating to say than, "Er – not sure. Might do."

He peered at me, then snapped his fingers and grinned his white-toothed grin. "Got it! You walked by the car park yesterday, you and that blonde bird!"

And I said, mentally kicking myself for sounding so stupid, "Oh, yeah," and thought, it *would* be Chloe he really noticed!

I said, "Her name's Chloe," and hoped he'd ask mine. He didn't, just grinned again and said "Cool!" And then, as an afterthought, added, "I'm Ash. Short for Ashley."

"Amber," I said.

"Amber. So, are you two from round here?"

"Muswell Road," I said. "Chloe's from Park Rise." And then I thought maybe I shouldn't have given out Chloe's details, so I clammed up.

"So, Amber," he said, "fancy a coffee while we're waiting for the wash?"

My heart was thumping. Surely this was an opportunity not to miss, fallen right in my lap. He seemed nice. I've noticed that boys are often nicer when they're away from their mates and not having to look big. I usually go back to the salon for twenty minutes while the towels wash and do some clearing up, then go back to get them dried and fluffed up. Bev is lovely but I don't know what she'd say if I went swanning off with a boy during work time. Reluctantly, I said, "Sorry, can't. I'm working."

He didn't seem too disappointed. I guessed he'd only been looking for a way of passing the time. But then he said, "D'you fancy a party later? It's for my mate's birthday, round at his place? You and Blondie?"

"Chloe," I said. My mind was working furiously overtime. Would Chloe come? Would Mum and Dad agree? Oh, they had to! I just couldn't pass up a chance like this.

I said, "OK, thanks. What time?"

"8.30-ish? 72 Briary Close. You'll enjoy it. Nice hair, by the way."

He'd noticed! I felt my cheeks grow pink. He put his hands in his pockets and sauntered to the door, pushing it open with his shoulder. "I'm off then. See you later, babe."

And he was gone, leaving the door swinging behind him.

My mind was in a turmoil. I got through the rest of the morning somehow, wondering if he'd be there when I went back for the towels. He wasn't; his machine was standing empty and silent. He'd been and gone. Never mind, I told myself, I'll see him tonight!

First off, I had to contact Chloe. I phoned her the minute I finished work. She sounded doubtful. "A party? What kind of party? Ash? Who's he? One of those bikers? Are you sure it's OK?"

"It'll be fine," I told her. "A *birthday* party, for goodness sake! His family'll be there and all. Please say you'll come! Mum and Dad will let me go if you're going as well."

She agreed, reluctantly, to ask her Dad and Aunt Sue. I hurried home to ask my parents. Of course Mum gave me the Spanish Inquisition. What party was this? What was the boy's name? I didn't know, so had to say he was a friend of Ash.

"Ash? Who's Ash?"

"Ashley," I said, and added, "Ashley Wilkes," as a name popped into my head, only later remembering that he was a character from the old film *Gone with the Wind*.

Mum didn't twig at all. "Wilkes? I don't know any Wilkes family in Briary Road."

"Mum, you don't know every single family in town."

"Don't be cheeky, Amber. Did you say Chloe's going with you?"

"Yes."

"Well, I have a lot of respect for her dad and her aunt, so it must be OK. But no staying late. Dad will pick you both up at half ten."

"Mum! We're not kids!"

She gave me a look. "That's a matter of opinion. Ten thirty."

Well, it was that or nothing. I was dreading that Mum would want to ring the boy's family to check on details. But she left it at that.

When I called Chloe back she said she'd had a similar conversation. "They only let me go because you're going, and you have sensible parents."

"We've got to be picked up, but we'll make the most of the time we have," I said. "Now, what are we gonna wear? Can you come round and we'll try on some gear?"

"Have you forgotten?" said Chloe. "We're going round

to Willow's this afternoon. Annie and Holls have been going on about that diary she's been reading and it sounds really interesting. I want to read it myself and find out what happens."

I groaned. I had forgotten. But I knew Chloe wouldn't be put off; old diaries are her kind of thing.

"OK, just for an hour or so. But we've got to leave time to sort out what we're wearing." A thought struck me. "Maybe Willow'd let us borrow some of her cool stuff?"

"Maybe," said Chloe. "I wish they were all coming too."

I was rather glad they weren't. Being part of a group is great, but there are times when a girl likes to branch out a bit and have some sort of life of her own.

four

All the other girls were already at Willow's, except Rachel, who had some family thing over the weekend. Annie and Holly were all agog waiting for us so we could all read the famous diary together. Personally, I thought it was a bit of a waste of time. It was a tatty little notebook, centuries old. I'd rather have hung out with Chloe and got ourselves geared up for the big event later.

Of course, we had to tell them about the party. We

tell each other just about everything, and I must admit I wouldn't really like us to have secrets from each other. I was a bit reluctant though. I felt we might get the Third Degree from Willow, and I was right.

"You mean, you picked up some boy in the *laundrette*? And agreed to go out with him, just like that?"

"No! I didn't pick him up! I'd met him before. Kind of. He invited me and Clo to his mate's birthday party, that's all. At his house, with his family and all. They're local people."

Willow didn't look convinced, and I began to feel a bit miffed. She was a fine one to talk anyway, the way she and Jay had latched on to one another from the word go. Obviously she's a mind-reader, because she said, "It was different with me and Jay. He was with a responsible team, and he's a Christian."

"So? There's no law against being friends with people who aren't Christians, is there? It's only a party!"

I was getting steamed up, and the others were looking uncomfortable. Perhaps Willow thought she had annoyed me, because she added soothingly: "Well, I hope you have a nice time. Would you like to borrow something to wear? I've got a really nice new black top."

Peace reigned again. I picked out a really cool top, and Chloe borrowed a dress. We all settled down on the bed and chairs, and Willow picked up the diary. She explained that it was written by a girl called Grace over a hundred years ago, and war had just broken out. She was writing about her older brother.

<u>*Aug 31st*</u>

Since the incident on the day of the parade, Will has been very moody. It is a huge insult to be presented with a white feather, indicating that the person receiving it is a coward for not being in uniform. The girl was a stranger, she wasn't to know Will is too young to enlist as he is so tall and well-grown and looks older. The incident upset him very much. He said to me a day or two later, "Gracie, I would give anything to be going to France."

I felt a cold chill, and was so glad he was not, although I did not say so. The same day, I saw him take his cornet case out to the barn to practise. He does that sometimes so that he does not disturb the family. I like to hear him, so went and listened outside the big doors. He was playing a haunting piece, sad and lonely and somehow piercing the heart. I told him I'd heard and he said it was the "Last Post", a solo they play at the end of the day and at the burials of soldiers killed in battle. I felt that cold shiver again. He said eagerly, "I'm thinking they might take me into the army as a bandsman. I believe they have boy musicians younger than enlistment age." He looked at me with his eyes shining. "Gracie, they're having such adventures! It is all so exciting, new countries and a different kind of life. I can't wait to be there with them!" He did not seem at all afraid. I did not reply, but I felt afraid myself. I hope he will never enlist. They are saying the war will be over by Christmas, and I hope and pray it will be so.

Sept 7th

These are strange times indeed. Last week our letters were brought by a post lady, who is replacing our postman gone to the war. So many men have gone, from all walks of life. None of us can avoid getting caught up in the war effort. Even Mother and Carrie's mother are knitting for the men; socks and gloves and scarves for when the weather gets colder.

Sept 10th

My world has collapsed! I am not to go away to school after all. At least, not this year. Mother and Father want us to be at home, safe and all together. I cried and pleaded, and Father got cross and said I have been too much indulged. Mother says there will be plenty to keep me busy at home, with the harvest to be gathered and a shortage of our usual helpers now that the young and healthy men are gone. So now I will be helping at home for a year. Next year, when this stupid war will surely be over, I can perhaps think again about the Grammar School. I don't want to be a farmer's wife; I want a proper education.

Sept 20th

Such strange things happen these days. It is as though the world has been turned upside down. There is such a hatred of Germans that seems beyond reason. Whole pages in the newspapers are full of stories about the dreadful deeds that people of that nation are supposedly capable of.

Two girls from our school, Gretchen and Helga
Muller, have disappeared from our town with their
parents, who ran the bakery. Nobody knows where they
went. There are tales that the family were spies and
that they returned to Germany after they were found
out and a brick was put through the bakery window.
I know the part about the brick is true, for I saw the
jagged hole in the window and now it is boarded up.
But I can't believe it of the family.

Gretchen and Helga were two of Carrie's and my
best friends, and we would go to tea in their rooms
above the shop when we were small. They had dolls
from Germany with beautiful china heads and they
always gave us delicious pastries, fresh from the oven
and covered in sugar and cinnamon. But they are gone,
and nobody knows where.

<u>Sept 21st</u>

Aunt Lily has created a stir in the family yet again.
She has gone to France as a nurse, to look after the
wounded soldiers, of whom there are a great many.
Mother is shocked. She says Aunt Lily's own life will
be in danger, working in the field hospitals near to the
enemy lines. I admire Aunt Lily for her bravery, though.

We start barley harvest soon. I am reading while
I can, "Ivanhoe", which is my very favourite book.
There'll be no time later for reading or writing. It will
be hard, Mother and I helping in the fields as well as
the dairy and poultry work and the cooking and care
of the house. And two of our horses are gone! Ruby and

Captain have been taken by the army, for the cavalry and to pull the big guns and supply wagons. They paid Father a good price, but it has left us with only old Ben, who is not strong in wind and limb and no use to the army. I wept and wept to see them go. What a dreadful thing this war is! Whatever will happen next?

<u>Nov 2nd</u>

Such a terrible thing has happened, so bad that I can scarcely write of it. And yet I must, because writing is the only thing that brings a little relief and ease. Last week . . .

Willow stopped reading.

"What happened?" asked Chloe. "Don't stop, Willow, what was the terrible thing?"

I had started listening feeling slightly bored, but now I wanted to hear what came next as badly as anyone. We were all eager to hear the rest of Grace's story.

"I don't know," said Willow. "It stops there, at the end of a page, right in the middle of a sentence. The rest of the book is missing."

She held up the exercise book, tattered and a lot thinner than it should have been. "Sorry guys. That's all there is."

five

There was a chorus of disappointed protest from the others.

"Oh no, it can't just finish there!"

"Where's the rest of it?"

"We've gotta find out what happened!"

"Sorry guys," said Willow again. "There was obviously more, but it's not here. The book got damaged at some point in the last hundred years and half of it went missing."

Even I would have liked to hear more of what happened to Grace and Will, and the other people she wrote about. Chloe seemed near to tears. She had been utterly absorbed by Grace's story. Then she brightened up.

"Willow, the rest of it could be in that trunk somewhere, couldn't it?"

"It might," said Willow. "But there's so much stuff there it would take an age to sift through it."

"Not if we all helped," said Chloe. "If we all got together, divided the stuff into piles and went through a pile each, we might get it done."

"I suppose so," said Willow. "OK then, let's fix a date when we can all meet up. Maybe we could have a sleepover. And we'll do a big search operation."

"We'll get hold of Rach and see when she can come," said Holly. "Next weekend might be good."

I got up from the bed. "We'll have to get going, Clo. Lots to do before tonight."

"Oooh, the big night!" said Holly.

"Enjoy yourselves," said Willow. "But don't get too carried away."

"No, boss," I said.

"Full report tomorrow morning," said Annie.

Truth to tell, I was a little nervous of the coming event. At tea time my stomach was full of butterflies and I just couldn't eat. "It's OK," I said, when Mum tried to force-feed me, as mums always like to do. "There'll be food at the party. I don't want to be too full to eat when I get there."

"Which reminds me," said Mum. "Do you want me to take you in the car?"

Heaven forbid, I thought. Totally uncool to be dropped off like a little kid. "No thanks, Mum. Clo and I will walk down."

"Well, all right. But your dad will be picking you up. And the two of you stick together, and keep your mobiles switched on at all times."

"Yes Mum."

I took ages to get ready, even though my hair was done and my make-up only needed a touch-up. I did add a bit of extra mascara and eyeliner, for dramatic effect, and hoped I'd sneak past the make-up police, aka Mum, without comment. To make sure, I only applied half as much as I wanted, and took it along to add more when we got round the corner. Chloe and I looked pretty good when we set off together, me in Willow's black top and a stretch mini-skirt over black leggings, her in black leggings too with a floaty dress over. Both of us had cute new shoes, and we felt like the Business.

It was just getting dark when we arrived at Briary Road, and the house was all lit up like a fairground. We could hear the music long before we reached the door. When we knocked, it flew open and a guy we didn't know ushered us in.

"Hey! Come in and grab a drink. What'll you have?"

We found ourselves in a house crowded with people; the living room and kitchen were packed and bodies were spilling out into the hall. Music was pumping out at thousands of decibels and everyone seemed to have a drink in their hand. I recognised some faces from school, but Ash was nowhere to be seen. The boy who'd opened the door said, "I'm Joe, by the way. My birthday. And you are?"

We introduced ourselves rather nervously. He was steering us towards a counter with bottles and glasses. "What're you having?"

I looked helplessly at the drinks. They all looked alcoholic to me. I had the idea that maybe I could just hold a glass of something and make it last all evening, but I hadn't a clue what I should ask for. "Coke, please," said Chloe.

"Two cokes coming up," said Joe, and grinned. Then Ash appeared from somewhere. "Hey, ladies! How you doin'?"

He grinned his white-toothed smile, but it was directed more at Chloe than at me. Joe brought us cokes in glasses. I took a sip and looked round. This wasn't quite what I'd expected. For one thing, it was quite obvious that this was no family celebration. Joe's parents were clearly not around. For instance, they'd never have approved of the way their furnishings were being treated. People were putting down drinks on polished tables and leaving rings, and there were already bits of crisps and nuts being trodden into the carpet.

And apart from the crisps and nuts, there was no food to be seen. I hadn't exactly expected a tea-party with jelly and cup cakes and sausages on sticks, but I'd expected *some* food – pizza or something. Sipping my coke, I felt my tummy rumbling with hunger, and I was glad there was enough noise to cover it.

Chloe didn't look too happy. And I suddenly felt a stab of sheer misery. Ash had latched on to Chloe, trying to steer her away from me and off somewhere by themselves. It was Chloe he was interested in, not me. What an idiot I'd been to imagine anything else. Clo didn't like it; her eyes were wide and apprehensive and she was sticking to me like a leech. I began to feel that this whole thing may have been a big, big mistake.

Someone bumped into me and spilt my drink, which splattered all over a blue satin cushion on the sofa. "Oooh, sorry, I'll get you another," said the person; a tall, skinny lad with a nose-ring. A glass was pressed into my hand. I took a sip and spluttered.

"What is this?" I asked, but the skinny lad had moved on.

Ash was there though, and he laughed. "Vodka and lemon. What's the matter? Don't you like it? Go on, drink up! It'll help you relax."

I don't know what came over me, but I did. And it did. All of a sudden, the nerves and resentment cleared and I got this warm, fuzzy feeling starting in my head and spreading right through me. I finished the glass, had another, or maybe another two, and began to relax. Maybe this would turn out to be a good party after all.

"Amber!" hissed Chloe in my ear. "What are you doing? We can't drink! We're only fourteen, remember, way under age!"

I didn't see why she had to advertise our young age to the whole room. "Age, shmage," I said. "Now we're here, let's enjoy it. You have one."

She shook her head and seemed near to tears when I accepted another glass. The thought did cross my mind that maybe I shouldn't be drinking on an empty stomach. Or drinking at all. I had a sudden fleeting image of my parents' faces if they could see me. I took another sip to block it out. The room seemed very warm suddenly, the music too loud, thumping in my head, the colours of peoples' clothes swirling and mingling. Chloe and I found ourselves squashed on a small sofa with a couple of others, and Ash perched on the arm next to Chloe. He kept putting his arm round her and she kept pushing him away. In the end, she said, "Get lost, you creep!"

He got up and said "OK, Blondie. Suit yourself. Better watch out for your mate, if I were you. She looks like she's gonna throw up."

I wished he hadn't said that. Because, all of a sudden, I felt sick. Very sick.

"Amber," said Chloe. "I think I'd better call your dad."

"No, no," I said. "Shfine. Having a good time."

Who was I kidding? The warm relaxed feeling had gone, and I felt very miserable and very ill. I suddenly noticed the two girls who'd been with the bikers at the car park, looking across at me and giggling. I wasn't having that. I began to get up, but suddenly the room was spinning and my legs felt like rubber. I heard myself say, in a far-away sounding voice, "I think I'll just have a little lie down." And then the carpet was rushing up to meet me.

PART FIVE

Chloe's Story

DECEPTIONS

one

When I come to write my autobiography, I think I'll be tempted to skip over that Saturday night that Amber got drunk. It was very humiliating all round.

I thought Amber's dad would blow a gasket when he came to pick us up and saw the state of her. He could see at a glance that there were no responsible people in charge, and looked like he'd like to punch someone's face. But he kept his head, picked her up and bundled her into the car and thanked me for calling him. Amber had come round by then but was still very woozy. "She'll have a very sore head in the morning," he said grimly.

I hadn't really wanted to go to that stupid party in the first place, and was sorry I hadn't tried harder to persuade Amber that it was a bad idea. But I didn't think either of us had properly realised what it would be like. I don't think she meant to get drunk, and I certainly wanted nothing to do with alcohol – it was a drunk driver who'd caused the accident to my brother, resulting in a life-threatening condition. And I certainly didn't want to snog that creep Ash, who poor old Amber had been so taken with. We'd been totally stupid.

I went round to see Amber next morning straight after church. I felt I had to tell her mum how sorry I was about the predicament we'd got into. Amber's mum is a really nice person, but she was very tight-lipped as she listened. She said, "I agree it was a really stupid thing to do, Chloe, and I wouldn't have believed it of the two of you. You weren't honest with us, and you are nowhere near old enough to be drinking alcohol. Don't you realise the dangers? Anything could have happened – you could have been assaulted, or fallen and seriously injured yourselves. People your age have died as a result of alcohol poisoning. We certainly won't be allowing Amber as much freedom as we have been."

I felt tears come into my eyes, and she softened a bit. "I know you're sorry, Chloe. I just hope you'll both never do such a thing again. Amber isn't up yet, but you can go up if you like. And maybe you'd take up this jug of water and make sure she drinks plenty." She gave me a hug with the other arm as she handed me the water jug, which made me feel a bit better.

Amber's curtains were tightly drawn and she was still in bed. At least, I assumed it was her, because all I could see was a humped shape under the duvet with not even a head showing. I found a glass on the bedside table and poured water into it.

"Ams? How're you feeling? Do you want some water?"

There was a groan from beneath the duvet, and a reply that sounded like "Urrrgh!".

I went to the window and opened the curtains. A tousled head emerged from beneath the bedclothes, but not for long. After blinking for a second or two Amber pulled the duvet back over her head.

"Ams," I said. "Have some water. It'll help."

"Oooh!" said a muffled voice. "I think I'm dying."

"No you're not. It's a hangover."

Another groan. Then her face emerged, streaky with make-up. "My head! It's splitting! I think my life is over!"

"Don't be silly." I offered the glass and she had a drink and fell back on the pillows. "Mum really went ballistic."

"Well, I think we deserved it. We behaved like total idiots."

Amber shuddered. "You mean I did. Well, I won't touch alcohol again, that's for sure." She slumped down into the bed again. "I don't know how I'm ever gonna look anyone in the eye again. I've let everyone down, big time."

"Don't be such a drama queen," I said. "You'll get over it."

She looked up at me mournfully, all bleary-eyed and mascara-streaked. "I wish I could believe that."

To give her her dues, she didn't try to duck out of the repercussions. Her parents grounded her for a week, going nowhere except school and BB. She didn't complain. And that first afternoon at BB, she was quite willing to talk to Sadie and the girls about what happened. I think I'd have tried to avoid it, but Amber spared herself nothing.

"I was a complete dork," she said. "I mean, how stupid can you get? I wouldn't listen to Clo. I've let you all down majorly. And the worst of it is knowing I let God down. What on earth must he think of me?"

There were tears in her eyes, and it wasn't just the drama queen thing. Sadie reached over and squeezed her hand. "I'll tell you what he thinks," she said gently. "He loves you very much. He's sad that you're feeling so bad, and he's just waiting for you to come to him and say you're sorry. You won't ever forget – and you shouldn't – but hopefully you'll learn from all this and never, ever repeat it. And God will forgive you."

Amber was properly in tears now. "Do you really mean that?"

"Of course. And it's not just me saying it – listen to this . . ." She picked up her Bible and flicked through the New Testament. "Ah, here we are, 1 John, chapter 1, verse 9: '*If we confess our sins, he is faithful and just and will forgive us our sins and purify us from all unrighteousness.*'"

"And I can just start all over again?"

"You can. And remember, if any of you happen to do anything bad – and you probably will – just remember that verse. It's God's promise to us all. The minute you've sinned, don't run away from God, run *to* him. As soon as you can. Satan would love us to feel guilty so he can taunt us and tell us we're useless. Don't listen. Jesus brought forgiveness for every sin, past, present and future, when he died on the cross. Remember that."

Wow! That was quite some thought. We were all well impressed. And Amber looked as though a heavy weight had lifted from her shoulders.

I must admit I'd been a bit apprehensive about facing Dad and Auntie Sue after the party. Not that they'd have heard anything then – news does travel fast round here but not that fast. I didn't know whether Amber's mum and dad would have got in touch, but hoped they hadn't.

Anyway, I was feeling well guilty by the time Amber's dad dropped me off, although I hadn't really done anything wrong, and I expected to get the usual grilling from Auntie Sue, at least.

"How did it go?"

"Who was there?"

"Did anything happen?"

"What was it like?"

I hadn't a clue what I was going to say. But strangely, they didn't say much when I went in. Dad and Auntie Sue were both watching TV, and Peter wasn't about. Auntie Sue looked up as I opened the door, and said, "Oh, there you are dear. Did you have a nice time?"

Dad just glanced up and said, "Hello," and then went back to his TV viewing. There seemed to be a funny atmosphere somehow. I wondered whether Amber's mum had been in touch. But they didn't seem at all cross or concerned about me. I didn't hang about, just said I was going up to bed, and went, wondering what was up and trying to rack my brains to think whether I'd done anything else wrong lately.

It wasn't until next day, after I'd been to church and visited Ams, and we'd had lunch, that I got some light on the subject. It wasn't me that was in the dog house. It was Peter.

two

Peter is my brother, and he's two years and five months older than me. He's tall and dark and a bit of a brainbox, heading for uni in everyone's opinion. He's sporty as well, and a nice person. As brothers go, he has just about everything.

Except that he also has a potentially life-threatening condition. It's not his fault at all; in fact the way it happened seemed so unfair that it was hard to believe at first. Two and a half years ago he was on his way home from a football match with the rest of the team, when a drunk driver of another vehicle slammed into them. The drunk driver died, and there were other serious injuries, and an awful lot of blood.

Peter only had cuts and bruises, and he helped with first aid and was later commended by the police for his presence of mind. But contact with infected blood means he now lives with the threat of serious illness or worse hanging over him. All the time.

It was a bad time for us all after the accident. Peter was depressed and hopeless and we didn't know how to help. Then everything was transformed when he discovered new hope by asking Jesus into his life. Now he lives a pretty normal life, medication keeps him well and you wouldn't know anything was wrong, most of the time. Best of all, I've got my big bro back again.

I got the chance to talk to Peter on Sunday afternoon, when Auntie Sue and Dad had gone out into the garden. Auntie Sue has become a keen gardener, and wanted Dad's help in making a rhubarb bed. Peter grinned at me over the dinner dishes as they went out. "I see rhubarb pie on the menu any time now," he said.

It's our regular job to do Sunday lunch dishes. The meal had been a strained affair, everyone being polite and considerate, but it was obvious something was wrong somewhere.

"Whatever's the matter with them today?" I asked.

Peter paused for a moment, his hands in the suds. "It's not them. It's me."

"What do you mean?"

Peter swished the dishcloth around and pulled out a red-edged plate. "We had a bit of a difference last night while you were out."

"What kind of difference?"

Peter stacked the plate in the rack and took out another. "About what I do next. After GCSEs."

"But it'll be sixth-form and A levels, surely?"

He wiped the back of his hand across his forehead, dripping suds. "That was the plan. *Their* plan. Then uni. All mapped out."

"But I thought that's what you wanted."

"Well, maybe I did. And maybe I've changed my mind."

He had a funny kind of look on his face. Determined, maybe. Or stubborn, depending on how you look at it. I dried a couple of plates before replying. "You mean you're going to leave school this year? But what then? Get a job? Everyone says there's a shortage of jobs."

"They're always advertising for staff in the supermarkets," said Peter. I'll work all summer, and save. Then take a year out before A levels. Kind of early gap year. Maybe go travelling. Work as I go."

My heart gave a flip. I'd got so used to Peter being home, needing to be looked after. "Oh, but Peter! You couldn't. You're too young. And what if you got ill?"

He gave me an exasperated look. "That's what *they* were saying! Why not wait until after A levels like other people do! You'll get out of the study habit and not want to go back. (Dad.) You can't throw away all your hard work! What if you're ill, or have an accident? You hear such dreadful things these days! (Auntie Sue.) Much better to wait until you're older. (Both of them.) And so on and so on, blah blah blah!" He paused for breath. I carefully dried another couple of plates, thinking how to reply. Truth to tell, I could see Dad's and Auntie Sue's points. And it made me feel quite sick to think of Peter taking off to goodness knows where.

I stacked the last dry plate and Peter wrung out the dishcloth. He looked out of the window to where Dad stood with spade poised while Auntie Sue gave directions. Auntie Sue is Dad's elder sister, she's always bossed him around and nothing much has changed. Peter sighed. "I just want to see a bit of life, something different, instead of the same old. Have a bit of excitement and adventure. See some different countries and cultures."

I had the strange feeling that I'd heard those feelings expressed by someone else recently, but I couldn't think who or where. Peter turned and looked at me, folding his arms and leaning against the sink. "How about you, Clo? You OK about life and stuff?"

I was a bit surprised. Peter doesn't usually ask me things like that. "Yeah, fine, I think so. I just wish I could get going with my writing career though."

He grinned. "At least you know what you want." He was silent for a moment and then said, "Clo, do you remember Mum?"

"No. I don't think I do, really. I was only three when she died."

Peter nodded. "I do." He flopped down on one of the kitchen chairs and put his feet on the rungs of another. "And I think of her a lot more now, because you're getting to look just like her. Same hair, same eyes, same way of laughing. And she was just like you, always reading."

I felt a bit breathless, as though someone had squeezed me round the middle. I wasn't used to discussing my mum with anyone. But suddenly, I wanted to know more. "What kind of books?"

"Well, I don't know what kind she read to herself. I was only a little kid. But I do remember her reading to both of us at bedtime. We'd all cuddle up together, and she'd read *Winnie the Pooh* and *Green Eggs and Ham* and *The Very Hungry Caterpillar*. *Barbar* was your favourite. But you always fell asleep half way through. She taught me to read, even before I started school. By the time I got there, I was way ahead of everyone else."

I was silent, surprised to find my eyes were misting over. I'd looked on Auntie Sue as my mother figure for so long that I often forgot I'd had my own mum once. And that she'd loved books, like me. Suddenly, I was determined that I'd make a go of my career as a writer. If my mum could see me, I'd make her proud.

Peter got up and yawned and stretched. "Well, I'm off to see if Matt and Baz want to hang out. What're you up to this afternoon?"

"Not sure," I said. "Maybe catch up with my mates, too."

I went upstairs, slowly, thinking hard. All of a sudden I felt lonely. Last night's party had been a mistake, big time. I couldn't talk about it to Auntie Sue or my dad, but I felt my mum would have understood. I wished she was still here.

However, I had my good friends. First off, I'd ring round and see if any of them wanted a mosey round town this afternoon. I was clicking on Rachel's number when something came to my mind. I remembered what Peter had said about excitement and adventure and how familiar the words had sounded, and where I'd heard similar ones before. It was in the journal that Willow was reading to us, where the girl Grace was writing about her brother, a boy of Peter's age who was desperate to go to war.

three

Our town is not exactly a hive of activity on a Sunday afternoon. Most of the shops are closed, and some of the restaurants and cafés are too, during the winter months. In summer there are visitors about and a bit more of a buzz, with some of the cafés putting tables and chairs out on the pavement under parasols, continental style.

This time of year it's a bit dreary really, although the spring flowers do look cheery in the parks and gardens. Annie was the only person I could get hold of. Rachel had a family thing on, Holly was out with her parents, Willow was on a Skype date with Jay, and Amber was still frail and recovering from the hangover. Annie and I walked round the park, looking at the ducks and commenting on their daft behaviour, and I found myself talking about my mum. Annie is easy to talk to; she's kind of sensitive and caring, and doesn't usually make judgments or tell one what to do. Not that the others do necessarily, but, well, they all have their opinions and sometimes less is more.

She listened sympathetically as I told her what Peter had said at lunch time.

"It's funny," I said as we headed back into town. "Now that I know Mum loved books, like me, it makes me really, really want to be a writer. I mean, I wanted to before, but it confirms it somehow. Maybe she wanted to be a writer too, but never got the chance, before she died. I just wish I knew how to get started."

"Bit of a busy time just now, exams and options coming up," said Annie thoughtfully. "But then, like Miss Miller says, if you really want to do something, you'll make the time to do it."

"It's not so much time," I said. "It's knowing how to start. I'm not daft enough to think I'll write a blockbuster best-seller straight off. I know you have to start small. I did that article for that posh *County* magazine, and they said it had potential, and to try other things with them. But I don't know what."

We were passing one of the coffee shops, the Coffee Corner. It was closed, but we were looking in at the chrome and lime green chairs and tables when an idea suddenly struck Annie. "Food reviews!"

"Pardon?"

"Food reviews. You know, reports of the different local cafés and restaurants."

I thought about it. "You mean, I'd have to go and have a meal in all the restaurants and cafés and then write about them?"

"Yes. It would be fun. You'd get to try all the places, and you could have a star rating system. There's loads of places in town. Send it to that *County* magazine. The Chloe Wright Guide to Local Eating!"

I thought of the eating places I knew, the five or six coffee shops, the two or three rather posh restaurants, half a dozen others, the pizza place, the sandwich bar, the Chinese, the fish and chip shop. I'd have to have an awful lot of meals out! The thought made me feel a little queasy, just after a big Sunday dinner. And what if people didn't like what I'd written about their places? If I wrote one iffy review I wouldn't dare show my face in that place again, plus I might get barred from all the others! Annie looked at my doubtful face and tried to be encouraging.

"It would be a good laugh! We'd come with you. Look, there are two right here in this street."

There were two places almost next door to each other; the Coffee Corner and Sasha's Sandwich Bar. Both were closed, thank goodness, or Annie might have insisted we go in and start right away. Dawdling past and taking notice, I saw a small place sandwiched between the two that I hadn't really noticed before, or maybe it was just that something new was going on there. To distract Annie from food reviews, I said, "Look, what's this about?"

There were a few mounted photos in elegant frames on stands in the small window, and a notice which said,

"Marina Mayfield's Model Agency. Child models wanted for catalogue and photographic work. Boys and girls up to fourteen years. Photographic appointments each evening between 5pm and 7pm, for the first week in March."

"Beginning tomorrow," said Annie. We looked at the photos, mostly of angelic-looking children in trendy gear.

"Then again," she went on thoughtfully, "you could do that."

I looked at her in astonishment. "What, go in for being a child model?"

"No! I meant, you could interview the people who are taking their kids for auditions. Find out about their ambitions and the kind of work they want to do. Writers have to do a lot of interviewing."

"I don't think the model agency people would think much of that," I said dubiously.

"Of course they would! It would all be good publicity. For you and for them."

I chewed this over as we walked on, half-listening to Annie's plans for me. I didn't think I was the best person to be an interviewer, being on the shy side. I do like talking to people though. And I would love to write up the results of an interview. I was wavering.

"I'll come with you," offered Annie. "We could go right after Beech Bank, tomorrow."

"I'll think about it," I said. "Don't mention it to the others though. I don't think I could cope with any more advice."

So there we were, the next evening just after six, having left BB a little earlier than usual and phoned home to say we'd be a little late. It all felt a bit hush-hush and rather exciting. The door to the place was open now, leading to a hallway with a flight of stairs, and a notice pointing upward that said "Photographic Sessions This Way".

The stairs led to a biggish room a bit like a doctor's waiting room, with a desk at one end. Already there were several hopefuls waiting, mostly mums with kids in tow.

"Go to the desk and explain what you're doing," said Annie, pushing me forward.

I wasn't quite sure myself what I was doing. I approached the desk nervously. The young woman behind it had a pointy kind of look, thin pointy face, pointy nose, short hair gelled up in spikes, and long pointy nails painted lilac. I couldn't see her feet, but I would have bet anything she was wearing pointy-toed shoes. She had lilac-rimmed glasses and gave me a pointed kind of look over them. "Name, please."

"Er, Chloe Wright," I said, and began to explain my purpose, but she waved a hand weighed down with massive silver rings and said, "Take a seat, please," then turned and began tapping her laptop keyboard.

There was nothing else for it. We found a seat and meekly sat down.

"We'll just have to play it by ear," said Annie.

I pulled out my pen and spiral-bound notebook and ventured a nervous look at the people waiting for their turns. I could hear a murmur of voices from an inner room, presumably the photographic studio. There was a subdued buzz of talk in the waiting room. I was beginning to kick myself for being so easily persuaded into things I really wasn't sure about. The party on Saturday night, and now this. I wished I was still at Beech Bank. Or at home. Anywhere but here.

four

I looked around at the other people in the room. There were a couple of young kids, a boy and a girl, maybe four or five years old, both of them white-blonde, blue-eyed and angelic looking. I'm not sure if they were twins, but they might have been. They were in matching outfits, blue velvet, the boy in a waistcoat and trousers, the girl in a dress, as though they were going to a wedding or something. Their mum kept adjusting the collars and picking off bits of fluff. I felt sorry for the poor kids, who looked bored to death and kept whining about being hungry and wanting to go to the park, or needing the toilet, and their mum was looking frazzled.

There was another mum with a very photogenic little mixed-race girl, sitting very still and looking around with big dark eyes. A bored-looking boy was swinging his legs and fidgeting, with an older lady who was probably his granny. And a couple of girls I recognised as being in Year Seven at school, with the mother of one of them. They weren't in school uniform but we were, and they looked embarrassed to be there, and avoided any eye contact with us. I was embarrassed myself.

"Get talking to someone," hissed Annie in my ear.

I tried to choose. Not the Beechwood High girls, they'd die from the cringe factor and probably so would I. The grandma? She caught my eye and glared over her specs. I didn't think she'd be co-operative. The mum of the blue-velvet duo was coming to the end of her tether, I could see. It would have to be the dark-eyed little girl and her mum.

I cleared my throat and started to get up, clutching notebook and pen. Then the door from the inner room opened and a mum with a young child came out, closely followed by another lady holding a clipboard. She scanned the waiting people, looked closely at me for a moment, consulted her notes, had a brief confab with the pointy person and then said, "Chloe Wright, please."

I was conscious of several pairs of unfriendly eyes turning towards me as I got up. A murmur of complaint rose in the room.

"Erm, excuse me, I think we were next," said the mum of the blue-velvets, and there was another general murmur. I didn't blame them, they'd all been there before me. I said, "I think there's been a mistake. In any case, I'm not . . ."

But before I could say any more the clipboard lady

strode forward and repeated, "You're Chloe Wright, yes?" and when I nodded, she took my arm and led me into the inner room. I looked over my shoulder and saw a startled look on Annie's face, then the door closed behind me.

There were bright lights at the far end of the room, from the cameras, I supposed, and a dim shadowy figure moving about who I supposed was the photographer. The lady with the clipboard sat herself down at a desk. She was middle-aged, grey-haired, bespectacled and homely looking. Presumably this was Marina Mayfield herself.

"Now then, Chloe." She peered appraisingly at me over her glasses and smiled encouragingly. "Yes. Blonde, good bone structure. Slim. School uniform, I see. Not necessarily a disadvantage. We'll do some shots of you as you are, then maybe a change of outfit. Mostly for catalogues, you understand. You won't mind popping behind the screen and changing into leisure wear? Maybe swimwear?"

I felt dumbstruck. She'd got the wrong end of the stick entirely. I didn't want my photo taken. And no way was I popping behind a screen and taking my clothes off.

She was saying, "Just undo another couple of buttons on your top, dear, and let your hair fall forward. Oh, and a nice big smile."

I found my voice. "Er, there's been a mistake. I'm not here to be photographed. I'm . . . I'm actually doing a report."

The smile disappeared. "You're what?"

"A report. For a local magazine. Interviewing prospective

models about their ambitions . . ."

There was suddenly an atmosphere of tension in the room. The woman looked towards the man behind the lights and muttered something. She got to her feet and looked daggers at me.

"Please leave. At once. We have nothing to say."

There was hostility in her eyes and her voice. I turned to the door, heart thumping, wanting nothing more than to get out of there, fast. I went over to where Annie sat and gathered up my coat and bag.

"Come on Annie, we're going."

"But . . ."

I couldn't get out of there fast enough. As the door of the room closed behind us, I was sure I heard the grey-haired woman say to the people still waiting, "I'm very sorry but there will be no more photographic sessions today." And a buzz of disgruntled voices replying.

"What on earth was all that about?" asked Annie when we were down the stairs and out on the street. My heart was still pounding. "Not sure. But I didn't like it. Something's not right somewhere. Let's go home."

I really didn't know what to make of this encounter, but didn't have long to wait until all was revealed. By the next day, Marina Mayfield's Model Agency was splashed all over the local TV news. The "studio" had disappeared overnight. Pictures of the grey-haired woman and the spiky-haired one flashed onto the screen, recognisable but with differences – the glasses and grey hair of the older one had disappeared and she looked much younger, and the spiky-haired one had long dark tresses. There was also a man, who must have been the mysterious photographer.

It seemed they'd been moving from place to place, renting premises and photographing children for supposed catalogue work. Parents had paid large sums up front for glossy photo prints that never materialised. And there was something far more sinister. There'd been reports of photos of some of the children appearing on Internet sites all round the world, used without permission and for who knows what sleazy purposes. It seemed that the mother of the blue-velvet kids had smelled a rat and reported them to the police.

"My goodness!" said Annie. "To think we nearly got involved in all that!"

The thought was already giving me cold shivers. The other girls were well impressed when they heard our part of the story.

"Fancy you braving a gang like that and getting them banged to rights," said Rachel.

I felt I had to put her straight on that. "I don't think they've been banged to rights yet. By the news reports they're still on the run. And I didn't exactly 'brave' them. I was scared stiff. And I didn't even know they were crooks!"

"Yes, but you got them rattled and blew their cover," said Amber, who watches too many police dramas. "Chloe Wright, Gang Buster!"

"Maybe that's how you should start your writing

career," said Annie. "Revealing injustices, exposing crooked things, protecting the innocent."

I shuddered again. "No thanks. A bit too exciting for me. I'd rather do the food reviews." All the same, the episode gave me a lot to think about. I'd heard the expression "the pen is mightier than the sword", though I didn't know who'd said it. Maybe I could use my writing skills to do real good in the world, to bring hope and courage, to stand against wrong things and uphold the right.

Then again, I also had the feeling that there might be the plot of a good novel in there somewhere . . .

five

Peter poked his head round my door as I was stuffing things into my backpack. "You off somewhere?"

"Yes, Willow's. We're having a sleepover."

"Oh, right. Well, just thought I'd let you know I'm all sorted now."

I zipped up the backpack. "What do you mean?"

"Well, I had a good talk with Rod the other night, and he came up with a plan. There's this kind of outdoor project going on in Scotland, it's called "Living Green". Where people learn to live off the land without destroying it, build timber houses from the trees that have to be thinned, create an environment that's sustainable without using up the world's resources. It's on all summer, lots of people my age are going. Rod knows the guy in charge and thinks he can get me on it."

He looked all excited and raring to go, quite different from the moody person he'd been all week. I'd been praying for something to change, and it looked like this might be the answer. I said, "Sounds great. But how about your other plans?"

"Well, maybe the travelling can wait a couple of years. If I can do something different over the summer I guess school won't be too bad afterwards."

"And the olds are OK with it?"

He nodded. "Dad thinks it's a good idea! Auntie Sue says I'll have to take plenty of thermal underwear, watch out for insect bites, and have plenty of diarrhoea pills along, what with compost loos and lack of proper sanitation." He laughed, a sound I hadn't heard all week. "Anyway, bring it on! Can't wait!"

He disappeared and I sat on the bed for a moment, breathing a silent thank you to God. A load had lifted.

At Willow's, getting our sleeping arrangements organised was no easy matter, when there were six of us sharing one room. Rowan was staying with Harry at Annie's house, so a couple of us could have gone in his room if we'd wanted to. But none of us did. Most of the fun of a big sleepover is all being together. Admittedly, the room was quite large.

In the end we decided as follows: Willow and Annie to share Willow's bed, as they are the two skinniest, and the bed is a bit larger than an ordinary single. We did toy with the idea of pushing the bed against the wall, and then the six of us all sleeping side by side across the two beds, upper parts on the bed, legs on the chair bed. But it didn't really work when we tried it; the chair bed was lower and our legs dangled uncomfortably. Besides, the ones in the middle thought they'd be too squashed, me especially as I get a bit claustrophobic sometimes. So, I got the chair bed to myself.

Amber reckons she can sleep anywhere and is used to squashing up, so she had a mattress on the floor in the far corner. Rachel says she's used to squashing up too, which must be true with the number of kids in her house, but that her sister says she sometimes snores so she went next to the window on another mattress. Willow said we'd need the window open anyway, or we'd die of asphyxiation with six of us in the room, and she thought maybe the fresh air would help the snoring. That's only Willow's theory, mind you; no evidence to back it up.

Holly was left with the airbed in the middle, which I'm sure she's not used to, but which she was very good about. The airbed is the worst option of all, as it tends to squeak whenever you move, as well as very gradually deflating during the night, so you find yourself on the carpet in the morning.

Anyway, by the time our sleeping arrangements were settled, we were hungry, so we got pizza and hot chocolate to eat in the kitchen and then went back upstairs for the main business of the evening. All of us changed into our PJs. Willow opened the trunk and started pulling out armfuls of the papers and assorted stuff in there and arranging it in six roughly equal piles on the floor, or the beds, wherever there was room.

"Now," she said. "Each take a pile. Every so often, say every fifteen minutes, I'll give a signal and we'll stop and put everything we've looked at back into the trunk. That'll cut down on clutter. And every 45 minutes or so we'll take a refreshment break."

Such organization! "Can you remind us what we're looking for?" said Rachel, who was the only one who hadn't seen the diary before.

"Oh yes!" said Willow, and picked up the tatty old notebook by the bed. "It's the other part of this. Or the cover. There was a green cloth cover on it once. Or just a page or two if you find one with the same handwriting." She passed it round so we could all have a look. The handwriting was beautiful, and I wished I could have dipped in to the diary and read more. But it would have to wait.

"It's written by a girl called Grace Elizabeth Hebdon," Willow went on. "So if you see anything else with that name on, a letter or anything, put it to one side. Oh yes – and this must be Grace, I think. I found it in the diary."

She picked up a photo and handed it to me first. I gasped. It was a black and white photo with a white edging all round, very old-fashioned. But it was the girl in the photo who surprised me most. She wore a kind of pinafore over a dark dress, with black stockings and buttoned-up boots. But her face was Willow's to a T, even down to the wild cascade of curls, although Grace's were tied back with a ribbon.

"If you see any more photos with her in, save those as well," said Willow. I think she must be my great-great something grandmother. I wish I'd known about her when Granddad was alive. There's so much I could have asked. OK, guys, that's it. Let's get started."

"Yes boss," said Amber.

I found it quite interesting to begin with, looking at all the old stuff Willow's granddad must have been hoarding for centuries. There were old booklets and things like how to prepare for war, and what to do in case of an invasion. That was World War 2, of course, not the one Grace had written about, which was even further back in history. But there was no time to stop and read things, if I wanted to keep up. At the end of the first fifteen minutes, we all gathered up the stuff we'd sorted already and put it back in the empty trunk. Another fifteen minutes passed, and we were all getting a bit tired. The novelty was wearing off.

Amber yawned and stretched her arms. "I'm getting pins and needles, sitting on the floor."

"I'm going cross-eyed, looking at all this paper," said Rachel.

I was beginning to think there were better ways of spending a Saturday night myself.

"We might never find the missing bit," said Holly.

I saw that these mutinous murmurings were making Willow look a bit guilty.

"You're doing me a big favour, girls," she said. "But you don't have to carry on if you don't want to. It's quite a bit more boring than I thought it would be."

"But we do want to find the rest of Grace's story," said Annie quickly. "It was so interesting, and we'd just come to a mysterious bit."

"Tell you what," said Willow. "Let's have our refreshment break now, and then see how we feel."

That sounded like a plan and cheered us all up. It was a while since the pizza, so a coffee and a couple of choc chip cookies would go down well. We began to gather up the last lot of things we'd sorted. Then Rachel let out a yell.

"Hey! Look at this!" She held up a tatty exercise book, or part of one. The missing part! And, yes, the handwriting was the same.

"That's it!" said Willow, her eyes shining. "Well done Rach!" She took the book and examined it closely. "It *is* it! And yes, it carries on right where the other part left off. Nothing's missing."

We'd all forgotten that we were fed up and in need of refreshment. "Let's read it," said Amber. "What are we waiting for?"

"Better tidy up first," said Willow. "Well, a bit, anyway. Let's just put everything back in the trunk."

We got everything back in record time, higgledy-piggledy, but it didn't matter now our mission was complete. Then we got comfy on beds and mattresses.

Willow switched on the lamp. "I'll read for a bit. If I get tired, one of you can carry on. But I think we'll go right through, now we're all together. OK, guys? I'll start from the beginning of the last entry."

PART SIX

Grace's Story

DISCOVERIES

one

<u>November 2nd</u>

   Such a terrible thing has happened, read Willow, *so*
bad that I can hardly write of it. And yet I must, for
writing is the only thing that brings a little relief and
ease. Will has left home, and he is gone to be a soldier.
We finished harvest last week, and I cannot express the
relief we felt, to have all safely gathered in, even though
it is late. It has been constant work for weeks, and we
would scarcely have time to catch our breaths before
beginning the work to be done before winter comes, the
ploughing of stubble fields, the planting of winter crops,
the pig killing, the hedging and ditching. And all with
none of our usual help.

   On Sunday we went to church, the first time for
weeks we have been able to. All the talk was of war, the
parson spoke of our duties to those on the front line
and the prayers were for our nation and the sacrifices
we must make to defend her. Will was very nervous and
tense all the way through, like a tightly-coiled spring
longing to be released. In the afternoon he asked if I
wanted to go out to the barn to hear him practise. I

do like to listen, but usually he does not encourage me tagging along. Then, when we were out of earshot, he stopped and grabbed me by the shoulders and turned me to face him. "Gracie, there is something I need to say."

I felt my heart begin to hammer, he looked so white and strange, and the little birthmark by his left eyebrow standing out like a tiny butterfly. He didn't wait for me to reply, but said, "Gracie, I have joined the army!"

I felt my mouth drop open. "But – but – how? You are not old enough."

He gave me a little shake. "That doesn't matter. I went to the recruitment post yesterday evening, and lied about my age. They didn't question it. Many of the lads are doing it."

I thought of the tales that are coming out of France, of death and mutilation and terrible battles, and seized one of his hands and cried, "Will, no! You cannot go!"

"Too late," he said, with a strange gleam in his eye. "I've signed up. If I wait until I'm of age, it'll all be over and I don't want to miss the fun. We're going to give them a real trouncing, I can tell, you, and it will likely all be over by Christmas."

I didn't know what to say. I thought of Father and how much he depends on Will, and Mother, who will be terrified for him. I could only say, "When?"

"Today," he said, and pushed open the barn door. There just inside was a kitbag, all packed and waiting, and his cornet case beside it. "I'm off now, Gracie. I

waited until the harvest was in but I can't wait any longer. I want you to give them this." He pulled a folded paper from the bag and pushed it into my hand. "I couldn't face the scene there would be. I tried to explain in this." He paused and said, "Gracie, don't look so tragic. Try and be proud. That is what families need to do. They said they might use me as a bandsman."

"Does that mean you won't be carrying a gun?"

Another pause. "I don't know. I don't really know much about any of it. There'll be training first, I suppose. But I can't wait to be there, Gracie!"

I had to turn away to hide the tears on my cheeks. I know many families are proud of their sons and brothers going to war. But I can only feel a terrible pain, and fear, and an end to our life as it has been.

<u>Nov 8th</u>

These last few days have been truly terrible. I could not say a word to Mother and Father but gave them Will's note. I have been angry since he left, at having to be his spokesperson and the bearer of such news. How dare he leave me to deal with the consequences!

Mother and Father took the news as I'd expected, very badly. Both were shocked; it had not occurred to them that Will might take this action. Mother cried a great deal and Father was so angry that the anger I felt seemed like nothing. He says that Will has made his bed and must now lie in it, that he had counted on him to be there on the farm, and now what? So angry was he that he said Will is no longer any son of his and he will not welcome him home. Which made Mother cry afresh and implore him to be merciful. I did not dare remind him that many of the lads never do come home.

We are all in a turmoil.

<u>November 13th</u>

I'm ashamed to say that I escape to Carrie's home whenever I can. Mother and Father have quietened down, though Father is sticking to his vow that he will not welcome Will home. Mother has stopped crying, and is beginning to feel a little pride in her son. There is a poster up in town which says "Women of Britain say GO!", encouraging mothers and sisters to be proud of their young men.

But inwardly she has great fear and cries again when she is alone. She thinks I don't know, but I see it on her face. Which isn't often, with all the work to be done. Home is not the same any more, and so I go to Carrie's. She has no brothers, just three younger sisters. However, it was almost as bad at first, because Carrie cried as well when she heard. Then she was brighter and I wondered why, until she showed me a letter she'd had from our Will. It said he was at training camp, still in this country and quite safe, enjoying the life and the friendships and eating good food. It also said, "Keep an eye on our Gracie for me, and tell her I'll write to her and Mother soon. See you at Christmas, I expect!" And was signed, "Your affectionate friend, Will." Carrie wouldn't let me have the letter but put it back into her pinafore pocket.

*I must say she is rather smug about it, although
sometimes we are both overcome when we really stop
and think that very soon Will may be on the battlefields
of France, facing who knows what.*

<u>*November 20th*</u>

*There is a lighter atmosphere in Carrie's house,
although it is noisier, with all the little girls. They
all have their work to do, of course, like any farming
family, but there are times when she and I can almost
rise above the bad times we're in. The other day we
were talking about Aunt Lily, when Carrie said, "I
rather envy your aunt. Wouldn't it be a glorious thing,
to nurse our wounded boys and be doing something so
worthwhile?"*

*I was not so sure. Some of the wounded have such
horrific injuries, mutilated bodies and missing limbs.
"We are far too young, in any case," I said.*

*"So was Will," said Carrie, with a toss of her head,
fingering the note in her pocket. She sighed. "I'm sure
if we tried we could pass for older, too."*

*We were in the bedroom she shares with her sister,
Sarah. She went and stood in front of the looking
glass. I joined her. We stared at our reflections, two
girls in our everyday dresses and pinafores, black
stockings, mine with a hole in the knee, I noticed,
which must have happened on the way over, and sturdy
boots. Messy hair escaping from its ribbons. Typical
schoolgirls.*

Carrie sighed again, and then brightened. "Still,

if we put our hair up and had long skirts, we'd look different. Much older." She tiptoed to the door and listened at the head of the stairs. We were alone in the house, her mother having taken the other girls with her to feed the pigs and poultry and collect eggs. Carrie and I had promised to get tea ready, but she darted across the landing to her parents' bedroom and came back with a dark woollen skirt of her mother's. She took off her pinafore and pulled on the skirt, tying a stocking from her drawer around the waist to stop it falling down.

Her mother is by no means a stout person, but Carrie is very slender indeed. She pulled off her hair ribbon and piled her hair up on top of her head, sticking in some hairpins to keep it in place. The effect was startling. Gone was the little girl and in her place stood a young lady. She looked at herself with what I can only describe as a smirk.

A door opened and closed downstairs and we heard children's voices. Carrie tugged off the skirt in a panic. "Quick, it's her Sunday one!" Hairpins and tangled curls were falling higgledy piggledy round her face. I couldn't help but laugh. I came home feeling better for it. You don't hear much laughter in our house these days.

two

<u>Dec 27th</u>

Christmas was not a happy day for us this year. I couldn't help thinking of when Will and I were small, and hung up our stockings with such expectations on Christmas Eve, and were up before daylight to see what Father Christmas had brought. We would all go to church together, even Father, who only attends at Christmas, Easter and Harvest Thanksgiving, and then we'd have a big Christmas dinner, and much feasting and fun. This year, I dreaded it.

The week before Christmas has never been enjoyable, because of the unpleasant business of preparing geese for Christmas dinners. Almost as bad as pig-killing. Two dozen or more geese, and sometimes ducks and chickens as well, one day cackling across the farmyard on their way to the pond, the next, slaughtered bodies, and our wash-house and kitchen turned into a plucking and dressing station with all the attendant sights and smells. Stray feathers everywhere, creeping into every corner of the house, in our food, our hair and up our noses.

From an early age, Will and I had done our share of the plucking, with coarse aprons round our waists and a dead goose dangling head-down on our laps, while Mother and the workmen's wives worked on the even nastier business of taking out the innards and preparing the geese for someone's Christmas oven. One wondered how the house could ever be normal again, but, miraculously, it always was, clean and polished ready for the festive season. And I soon forgot all the nastiness when the roast goose was on my plate.

This year, it's been different. Less orders for geese, people have so many family members away and I suppose less heart for celebrations. But my help was needed even more than usual – ugh! And there was a gloom over our house because of the empty place at the table. Mother tried hard, but it was a struggle. The war has not been won by Christmas. Will is in France now and we have not heard from him, except to say he was going. I'm glad Christmas is over. I have no heart for it.

Jan 8th 1915

We've had a letter from Will, which was meant to have reached us before Christmas. It just said "Dear Mother, Father and Grace, I am safe and well and wish you a Merry Christmas and Happy New Year. Things are not so bad here. Trusting you are all well, your affectionate son and brother, Will."

I looked hopefully at Mother and said it did not sound too bad. She said, "Yes, but you have to read between the lines." She is determined to be gloomy at

the moment. I went to Carrie's with belated Christmas
boxes for her and the girls. She gave me a book called
"The Vicar of Wakefield" which I cannot wait to read.
She knows I love books. I also took Will's letter to show
Carrie, and she was put out because she has not heard
again from him. She took it from me and studied it for
ages, although it was such a short note, as though there
might be some hidden meaning somewhere. Then she
said, "I'm sure it must be worse than he says. You hear
such things."

I'm beginning to feel exasperated. She and Mother
are a pair at the moment. Why can they not look on the
bright side?

<u>January 12th</u>

Well, since writing that I'm not sure that there is any
bright side to look on. All the war news is depressing,
although we are constantly being told to keep our
spirits up. It's cold and miserable here, wet and short
dark days, not pleasant at all out of doors. It does not
bear thinking about our Will and the boys over there.
They have no buildings to live in at the front lines,
they sleep, eat and live in deep trenches dug in the
ground. They only leave when it is time to go "over the
top", that is, when they have to go out and attack the
Germans. It has rained there as much as here, or more,
and there must be so much mud. I am used to mud,
goodness knows, but I have a dry house and warm fire
and feather bed to sleep in. How awful it must be to
have no such comforts.

January 20th

At Carrie's house again today. She was in a thoughtful mood. She said, "Last Sunday, in church, when they were saying prayers for our soldiers, I suddenly felt that I should be praying more myself. Like the vicar said, we don't have to be in church to pray. Anyone can, at any time, anywhere. So I made up my mind I would devote myself to prayer. Miss Simpson used to have that saying, 'More things are wrought by prayer than this world dreams of.' So I am getting up earlier every morning to pray for an hour, for this horrid war to end and for W – for everyone to come home safe."

I knew she had been going to say Will. And I was astonished at what she proposed to do. To get up an hour earlier, on freezing cold dark mornings, before the fire had been lit! I have to admit I don't feel equal to such an undertaking myself. But I admire her resolve. Though a cynical part of my mind thinks she will not keep it up for long.

January 23rd

We have had another letter from Will, a much longer one and so strange. Something happened on Christmas Day that was unexpected and like a miracle. Instead of the usual shelling and firing at each other, which happens every day, he says: "There were just a couple of shells, aimed high, as if wishing us the Compliments of the Season. No more shots were fired.

"Then someone said the Germans and British had begun calling to each other across the lines, and before

we knew it, men were climbing out of their trenches, from both sides, and meeting each other and shaking hands, as though they were at some social event. Then they were singing songs, English and German, and making jokes and talking as though they were the best friends in the world. I talked to a lad named Ludwig, about my age, he gave me some sweets and I gave him a chunk of Mother's Christmas cake. (Thank you for the parcel, Mother!)

"All along the lines they were exchanging sweets and chocolate and cigarettes. It was the strangest thing. No shots were fired that day. Those Germans, most of them, are lads just like us.

"I trust all are well at home. Yours affectionately, Will."

Of course, I wasted no time in showing this to Carrie. She was jubilant! She went quite pale, so her freckles stood out, and said, "You see? It is a miracle! This is God answering prayer!"

Well, I said nothing, but I had my doubts. I did not say so, but it occurred to me that this had happened before Carrie began her prayer vigil. It was wonderful that it happened, but how much can be attributed to prayer I am not sure. They were back to shooting and shelling each other the next day. And why did God let this war begin in the first place? I have so many questions.

But, as I have said before, I cannot help but admire Carrie. She's still getting up early to pray.

three

<u>*February 1st*</u>

*This is such a long, dreary winter. I've never known
one like it. It just goes on and on, the same every day.
All the animals are inside now, of course, which makes
for an endless round of feeding, watering and mucking
out. I am called upon to help Father with the work, in
the absence of Will, and I go about with the stink of
cow and manure clinging about me, on my boots, my
clothes and in my hair.*

*I long for a bath every single night, but it can only
be managed on Saturdays, and such a palaver! Kettles
to be boiled, the tin bath brought in from the wash-
house and put before the kitchen fire, a clothes horse
put up with the towels and my nightgown warming
upon it. Then Mother and Father retire to the parlour
while I take my bath. I make it last as long as I can,
washing my hair with soft soap and pouring jugs of
water over my head to rinse. I stay in until the water
cools.*

*It's such a good feeling after a bath, but of course it
doesn't last. Mother tells me I should be grateful I am*

*not one of a large family, with all taking their turns in
the same bath water. When I am grown-up I will have a
bathroom and bathe every single day! And I will not be
a farmer's wife either!*

<u>*February 5th*</u>

*It's a long time since we heard from Will. Things are
bad over there. They say there's thick mud everywhere
and rats in the trenches. Two of our boys from the
village have been killed, Tom Wainwright and Martin
Wicks. That was such a shock: it made everything
seem real. They are lads I've known all my life. We are
beginning to dread the arrival of the post lady. News
of a death in action comes by a telegram from the War
Office. There's always a sense of relief when she hasn't
come that day, or when she's only brought ordinary
letters. Mother says she is glad there is so much to do,
it leaves less time for thinking and worrying.*

Why, oh why, can this war not come to an end?

<u>*Feb 17th*</u>

*Carrie came to visit today. We are too busy or too tired
to visit much these days, besides, tramping across
muddy fields in winter is no fun. She told me there
is an organization called the Women's Forage Corps,
which will be sending women to work on the land when
the spring ploughing and planting begins, to help
short-handed farmers. And that the women will wear
trousers! I couldn't believe it, but she has seen a picture
in the newspaper, and it showed a woman in a smock,
trousers, and boots, like a man. We talked about it for*

a while, wondering how it would feel to be dressed like that.

"I think I would like it," I said. "Imagine the freedom of not having skirts, and being able to run, jump, climb and do things boys do."

Carrie was not so sure. "But not very ladylike, I think."

"Who cares?" I replied. "I hope it happens in other circumstances, not just farm workers. Just think – in another twenty years maybe every woman and girl will be able to wear trousers without creating a scandal."

Carrie said she doubted it. Then she came to the real point of her visit, which was to see if we had heard from Will. I hated to tell her we had not. Her face fell but she was in an optimistic mood today. "Well, no news is good news."

I asked her if she still prayed for Will and the others, and she looked surprised and said, "Of course! We have to keep on!" and quoted a verse from Luke's Gospel, which says that, "men ought always to pray, and not to faint. And women too," she added.

I did not like to tell her of the doubts I often feel. Or mention Tom and Martin, our schoolmates, whose graves lie in some foreign soil. Sometimes I'm the one who finds it hard to look on the bright side. But I admire Carrie's faith.

<u>February 21st</u>

A letter from Will! In fact, two letters, arriving together, neither of them long. He says they are not often able

to get home letters out to be posted, so they are mostly
late, or several come at once. The first one says that he
is playing his cornet, sometimes, when they are able to
conduct proper burial services for their fallen comrades.
The thought made me shiver, remembering that time I
overheard him play the heart-rending notes of the "Last
Post" when he was still safe at home with us. But the
letter sounded cheery in general.

The second letter was more disturbing; he mentions
losing several of his close friends, and goes on to tell of
what we should do with his possessions at home in the
event of him not coming back. It was as if he'd realised
suddenly that he might not. Mother was quite stunned,
and said what if it was a premonition, and I had this
feeling of being punched hard in the stomach. But I
pulled myself together and tried to reassure her that he
was probably just homesick and having a bad moment.
But I cried when I was alone, thinking of how eager
he had been to go to war, and what an adventure he
thought it would be.

March 7th

There is talk that there will be another big engagement
to take place soon, at a place called Ypres. The soldiers
find the French names hard to pronounce, and call
it Wipers. I did not know where Ypres is, so Father
got the atlas and showed me. It is in Belgium, near
the French border, and is a strategic spot for military
purposes. There was a big battle there in the autumn
and Father says there will be more.

*I am glad to say Father has changed in his attitude
towards Will, and all the things he said about
disowning him have been disregarded as angry words
in the heat of the moment. Mother and I are so glad.
It comforts us and makes us feel that we are all united
again.*

*Spring is on the way, the snowdrops are flowering,
pussy-willow and lamb's tails have their powdery yellow
catkins, and there is just the first hint of green on the
tree buds. Strange that everything goes on and the
seasons change just the same whatever is happening in
the world.*

Willow paused in her reading, cleared her throat and
took a drink from her water bottle. "I'm getting croaky,"
she said. "Anyone else like to take a turn?"

Chloe jumped up at once. "I will, if you like."

"Thanks," said Willow gratefully, and handed her the
book.

four

<u>March 10th</u>

*We do not of course take a daily newspaper. As we are
farming people, we are obliged to do all the shopping*

we need to do on a Thursday, which is market day. I cannot imagine a life where one could walk out of one's front door and find shops just along the street. On Thursdays, Mother and Father take the pony and trap and drive the four miles to town, where everything we need for the week is purchased. Including a newspaper, which we all read avidly. Reading it, I am slowly realising that in many ways we are fortunate.

There are beginning to be shortages of some foods, as our convoys of merchant shipping are blocked or torpedoed, with great loss of essential supplies. Apparently two-thirds of our food in this country comes from overseas! Mother tells me we are fortunate on the farm, and I can see it for myself. We have all the milk, butter and cream we need (though it is very hard work producing it), we have our own potatoes and root crops, jams and preserves and bottled fruit, we grow our own vegetables and fruit and we have chickens, ducks and geese for meat as well as eggs, we keep a pig so have all the ham and bacon we need.

We can make bread if we need to, though it's very time-consuming and much easier to get it from the baker in town, although the new baker is nothing like as good as Herr Muller, who has disappeared. All we need to buy most weeks is flour, sugar, dried fruit and tea, candles and salt, with sometimes a few luxuries like sweets and coffee. So we are luckier than many. I still do not want to marry a farmer though!

March 17th

*Carrie has had a letter from Will! Not a very long
one, but she was so excited she came running across
the fields and into our yard, without a coat, although
fortunately it was a beautiful sunny spring day. She
was quite unusually flushed, a look which doesn't agree
very well with her freckles.*

*The letter read, "Dear Carrots, I am quite well
though several of the lads have been sick with colds,
coughs and dysentery, and two have trench foot and
have been taken to hospital. We lost twenty seven in five
days last week. I suppose it's springtime back home,
daffodils out and the hedges greening? You wouldn't
know it here, although sometimes we still hear the birds
sing. A blackbird was singing his heart out up on the
wire this morning. It reminded me of home. Thank you
for your letters. I am glad of them. Your friend, Will."*

*I suppose I should have been heartened by this
message but somehow it made my blood run cold. The
phrase "we lost twenty seven in five days", slipped in
amongst talk of flowers and birds, as though it was
nothing unusual. I suppose it is not. Every day more
lads die or are horribly wounded. I spoke to Edith
Slater in town last week; her cousin has come back
from the war, and has lost a foot. But, she says, the
worst of it is he is what they call shell-shocked, and
is not like the person who went away; he scarcely
speaks or takes interest in anything and has terrible
nightmares when he sleeps. And Will sounds so*

homesick.

I must be like Carrie, and be more faithful in prayer. Her faith in God seems to grow stronger by the day. When I spoke about it, she said, "Well, with everything in the world seeming in turmoil, it's so comforting to know that God always stays the same. And that he's promised he'll never forsake us."

"Then why did he allow this terrible war to happen?" I demanded.

She was quiet for a moment, and then said, "I think the war is to do with the wickedness in people's hearts. We have free will, don't we, and can make choices. If enough people, and especially the leaders of nations, choose to give in to greed and envy and hatred and fear, then dreadful things will happen. As they have."

Carrie is so wise, for someone not yet fifteen. And so steadfast. She is an inspiration. She does not show me what she writes in her letters to Will, but I am sure they must be a great comfort to him.

April 9th

It is Will's seventeenth birthday. And already he has been fighting for his country for five months, all through this dreary winter. Mother and I made up a parcel and sent it two weeks ago, but there is no way of telling whether or not the parcels always get through.

April 17th

A new weapon has been unleashed and it is a most fearful one. Poison gas! I read about it in Father's newspaper, though he tries to keep me from reading

*the war reports. I believe he still sees me as a little girl
to be protected. This gas is a terrible thing, it sears the
lungs and blinds the eyes. The men are being issued
with gas masks, there was a picture in the paper, they
make them look like some kind of strange and inhuman
monster.*

<u>April 29th</u>

*This morning was turning out day, when we let all the
cows and young cattle out of their winter quarters to
graze in the fields again. I am so glad to see this day,
and an end to the drudgery of forking fodder, carrying
water and shovelling manure. Though not as glad as
the poor beasts are themselves!*

*I couldn't help but laugh when I saw them emerge,
blinking in the bright light and looking bewildered, and
then suddenly realise they were free, and begin running
and leaping and bucking and galloping from one end of
the meadow to the other. Even the sedate old matronly
milking cows! And now they're having a wonderful time
munching on the new green grass and buttercups.*

<u>9th May</u>

*The "Lusitania" has been sunk, off the coast of Ireland,
taking with it 1,198 passengers and crew and all of the
cargo aboard. 761 people survived. The ship carried
war supplies as well as passengers. It is a great tragedy.*

<u>May 15th</u>

*Such news! It came with the post lady, on a postcard
marked Field Service, so obviously the post lady had
read it, and she handed it to Mother with a sympathetic*

look, but not too sympathetic, as she must have
delivered many worse. Mother had been expecting a
letter for so long that she almost fainted, though the
fact that it was a postcard came as a surprise. I took
the card from her and read it first. There was not much
written, just Will's name and details, and a printed list
of options to be crossed out, or not, as the case may be.
The only line not crossed out was "I have been admitted
to hospital wounded" and Will's signature, very shakily
written.

Mother and I both wept and trembled and held on
to each other, and Father came out from his papers to
see what all the fuss was about. We all read the lines
over and over, turned the card and read the address
side and tried and failed to decipher the postmark, but
there was no more information to be had. Father has
now harnessed the trap and gone into town to try to
get more details, though how he will get them I have no
idea.

Our minds are full of questions. What kind of
wounds has Will sustained? Has he lost limbs, arms,
legs, hands, feet? Has he been gassed? Blinded? Every
new thing we think of seems worse than the last. Father
says we must be thankful that at least he is alive. And
could write his signature. I don't know what to think,
my head is in a whirl. I must see Carrie and break the
news to her. May the Lord help us all.

five

Chloe put down the book and looked round at the others, who blinked, rather as though they'd been watching a movie and were coming back to reality. "Well, that's it."

There was a chorus of protest. "You mean the end?"

"It can't be!"

"It can't stop there!"

Willow picked up the book and pulled a face. "Sorry, guys, but it does. The diary ends right there."

"But we have to find out what happened to them all!"

"I know," said Willow. "It's really frustrating. But unless there's another diary hidden away somewhere, that's it."

There was a chorus of groans. "That means more searching, and we're not sure to find anything in the end. I don't think so!"

"Isn't there someone we could ask?" said Annie.

There was a tap at the door and everyone jumped. Willow's dad's voice said "Erm, I hate to intrude, Willow, but your mum has sent me up to see if everything's all right in there. You've all been so quiet. No giggling, no shrieking, no music. Unnaturally quiet. Is everything OK?"

"Fine, Dad, thanks," said Willow. "We've been reading something."

"Great," said her dad. "Something inspiring, I hope, and not one of those silly girly mags. See you all in the morning."

They heard retreating footsteps as he turned to go downstairs.

"Dad!" yelled Willow, shooting upright on the bed so suddenly that she almost sent Annie tumbling to the floor. "Dad, wait!" She scrambled from the bed and flung the door open.

"I'm such a numpty!" she said. "Why didn't I think of asking Dad before? It's his family, for goodness sake, and he's a humanities teacher and into history. He'd know if anyone would!"

By now the other girls had got up and crowded to the doorway after her. Her father stopped half way down the stairs, looking bewildered. As the light shone down upon his face, they could all see the small butterfly-shaped birthmark just above his left eyebrow. Willow remembered that Granddad had had one exactly the same. And she also remembered, with a flicker of excitement, that Grace had also mentioned a similar birthmark on Will's forehead.

"Dad," she said. "We're reading an old diary we found in Granddad's trunk. And we want to know what happened afterwards."

"I see," said her father thoughtfully. "Well, maybe I can help you there. I have a family tree somewhere. Who wrote this diary?"

Willow darted back into the bedroom and picked up the photo. "She did, I think."

Her father peered at the photo, raised his eyebrows in surprise, looked at his daughter and back at the photo. "Well. Quite a striking resemblance. This must be your great-great grandmother, Willow." He counted off the generations on his fingers. "Yes, that would be right. I've seen photos of her before, but never one at this age. Could almost be your double."

"I knew it!" said Willow triumphantly. "Could you show us the family tree, Dad?"

"I suppose so," said her father. "Why don't you all come down to the study. Delving into history, eh, a bit of a change from your usual kind of pyjama party."

"Yes Dad," said Willow. "Only it's called a sleepover these days. Come on, girls."

Everyone, pyjama clad, trooped downstairs and crowded into his small study. He opened a filing cabinet and searched through the files. Considering the higgledy piggledy state of the rest of the house, Willow obviously took after her dad when it came to neatness and orderliness. He pulled out some papers and spread them on the desk. He unfolded one, which they could all see was a family tree with the generations branching off across the page. Everyone crowded closer for a better look.

"Now then, let's see." His finger traced the names, going back through the generations of names and dates. "There's your granddad, and there are his parents and yes – there we are. William Hebdon and Caroline Clarke, married on April 4th 1921."

Several of the girls had been holding their breaths, and let them out in a sigh of relief. "Will and Carrie," said Chloe. "So he did come back from the war, and married Carrie."

"Do you know any more about them, Dad?" asked Willow.

He shook his head. "Nothing much, I'm afraid. Except that they seem to have had a large family, according to this." He pointed to several names coming directly after those of Will and Carrie.

"So we still don't know how badly wounded he was, or what happened to them afterwards," said Amber. "Or if they were happy."

"I think they were happy," said Annie.

Willow was looking at the chart with a little puzzled frown. She saw that Grace Hebdon was listed as William's sister. "I don't really understand," she said slowly. "Where does Grace fit into all this? And how come she's the one that looks so much like me?" She held up the photo. Her father laughed. "Oh, that's not Grace! That's Carrie. Your great-great grandmother, as I said."

Things were falling into place.

"It must have been Grace who took the photo of Carrie!" said Rachel.

"With her Box Brownie camera," said Holly.

"I remember Aunt Grace," said Willow's dad, surprising everyone. "Will and Carrie were gone before my time, but I do remember being taken to see Aunt Grace when I was a little boy. She was a very old lady, and quite a character. My dad used to tell some tales about her."

"What was she like?" asked Amber. Everyone was holding their breaths again. He'd actually met Grace, the girl who'd written the diary.

"Well, like I say, a bit of a character. As I recall, she went to university to study English, the first ever from the family. And went on to be a lecturer and professor herself."

"Wow! And did she get married? She always said she wouldn't marry a farmer!"

"I don't believe she ever did marry. She was living alone in a little house full of books when I met her. I was a bit in awe of her, but she was very kind, and gave me lemonade and ginger biscuits. And a book. She said it had always been her favourite."

"*Ivanhoe*?" asked Chloe.

"Yes," said Willow's dad. "I think I might still have it."

Everyone trooped back upstairs in thoughtful mood, remembering the two young girls who had lived long ago in a war-torn world.

"Imagine," said Chloe to Willow. "You're descended from Carrie! And Grace was part of your family too. You're lucky. They seem to have been two awesome women."

"Maybe you'll take after them and be awesome yourself one day," said Holly.

"I'm awesome already," said Willow with a grin. "All of us are. But just one thing: I might be the image of my great-great-grandmother, minus the freckles, but don't any of you dare take it into your heads to start calling me Carrots!"

More books in the
Beech Bank Girls series by **Eleanor Watkins**:

Beech Bank Girls – Every Girl Has A Story

Six teenage friends draw nearer to God and to each other in these fun, moving and honest accounts. Annie, Willow, Rachel, Holly, Amber and Chloe share their laughter, their fears and their secrets with each other and with us. Miracle and party included!

"I really enjoyed it and found it helpful at the same time."
– Claire

"I loved reading about the different girls' lives and how they struggled with different problems at home, at school and with their Christian lives. It also teaches more about God, like how he knows each and every one of us, he loves us all, listens to us and will help us with everything."
– Emma

Beech Bank Girls – Making a Difference

The Beech Bank Girls are back! Holly is in Australia, but Willow, Amber, Chloe, Annie and Rachel discover that they do not have to wait until their gap year to start helping people in need.

An interesting hike, a new culture on their doorstep, an emotional night out . . . the girls learn from some tough issues that they can make a difference right where they are and have lots of fun at the same time!

"A very exciting, fun to read, really well-written and easy to understand book. Looking forward to the next one!"
– Taylor

"When the girls get into bad situations or dilemmas they all get together and pray . . . makes you want to read more and find out what happens next." – Ellie

Beech Bank Girls – Christmas is Coming!

Christmas is coming! Along with the excitement, life holds its challenges for the Beech Bank Girls. Holly faces the reality of financial crisis at home; Rachel is worried about her sister; a sledging incident shakes the girls – and a very different nativity play brings home the true meaning of Christmas.

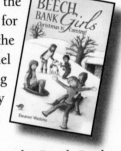

Family, friendship and faith issues – the Beech Bank girls face them together in this, their third book.

> "An amazing, heart-warming story about six normal girls who go through everyday situations, but at the end of the day they realise that the best solution is to turn to God. This story shows that God is an amazing father who really cares for us and our problems, no matter how big or how small they are. A definite 10/10."   – Ellie

> "A really interesting read and the author pulls you into the story."   – Sophie

London's Gone by **J. M. Evans**

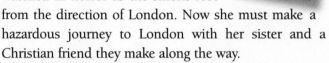

London has been bombed by terrorists. The government has been wiped out, there is widespread power failure, and throughout England riots have begun.

Maria saw the war planes fly over the home on the outskirts of London and watched in horror as the smoke rose from the direction of London. Now she must make a hazardous journey to London with her sister and a Christian friend they make along the way.

For Maria, the journey is also inside herself as she is forced to face issues that she has never had to consider before, and begins to discover a side to life she never knew existed.

A gripping drama for young people.

"I just couldn't put this book down."   – Gilly

"Very exciting, full of atmosphere."   – Eleanor

The Only Way by **Gareth Rowe**

When a mysterious, disaffected teenager meets the beautiful and mysterious Lily, he discovers a new way to live, the only way.

Later, when Lily's life is in danger, he is willing to risk everything to save her, but time and circumstances are against him. How can he live, if she doesn't survive?

"The girl is mysterious and it's good that you don't know much about her. The boy has quite a hard life; I liked the bit where he had to live off the land. The Christian side of the book is subtle; I think it would be helpful to someone who is unsure about their faith. This is a very good book with some exciting moments."　　　　　– George

"*The Only Way* is a moving, fast-paced, gripping and genius piece of writing. A 'must read' for everyone."
　　　　　– G. P. Taylor, *New York Times* best-selling author

Find all these books and more at
www.dernierpublishing.com

DERNIER
PUBLISHING